SKYE

Ophelia Finsen

Also by Ophelia Finsen:

Lovers of Old Films
This is Living
Society of Lost Causes
The Women of Jimanac

ISBN: 978-0-9559923-6-0

The rain was lashing. Whipping. Her brown curls were limp, darkened, sodden by rainwater. Hair tangled across her eyes. Her breath caught up in her throat. Her feet burned from the walking. Her legs were weak and her hands were shaking. After all these years she had got what she wanted.

He appeared out of nothing to her side. It was dark, only the moon and a small lamp left on the stone close by. He didn't trust the wind not to snatch away his words, and leaned in close to her ear. "I hear you've been looking for me."

She had. Many years had seen her lingering by the window. Praying for a word of news.

"What are you expecting?"

A line of rain water twisted down her forehead, into the corner of her eye and down towards her half-open mouth. She did not know what to say. She had never thought this far. What would happen when she arrived; when she had seen him.

He grinned. Two of his teeth were missing. "The moon is out," he whispered. "And nothing in your head can prepare you for what I will do."

An t-Eilean Sgitheanach

"I suspect this spray will kill me before it kills them."

"At least we shall die happy."

"I can think of better ways to go."

Ylva looked up at the sky and considered the grey clouds flecked over with light drizzle. The weather was set for permanency today. It was a shame because the previous two days had been glorious – both with the weather, company, activities, and that all consuming factor that seemed to take over all locals' lives at this time of the year – being midge-free. Of course it wasn't to last and the light rain had brought the speck-like flies back out in hazy, nipping waves of mist.

Dipping into her waterproof coat pocket, she took out a tub of homemade insect-repellent cream and dabbed some on her face as if she was protecting herself from the sun. It worked to a point, but Ylva had always found the best repellent for biting insects was alcohol. Whether it was that the taste of your blood changed, or you just stopped caring; the end result was the same, and on long summer evenings, it had worked.

It was the silence she couldn't get used to. The way you didn't notice midges until they were either dancing on your eyelashes or pricking at your skin. At least the mosquitoes in Sweden, where she had grown up, had the decency to make a sound, however irritating, before the attack. And unless you were right up north, they didn't appear in such apocalyptic clouds. On the other hand, the biting bugs in Scotland didn't kill you, whereas ticks in Sweden, for example could give you encephalitis. It was swings and roundabouts.

Agnes and Mildred, the two seventy-year-olds from Northumberland, were taking a break from their watercolours to douse each other in aerosol bug repellent purchased from a chemist in a part of the world where midges weren't a problem.

Agnes laughed and put the can in her rucksack. "Well, my dear," she said, turning to Ylva, "We are martyrs to our art."

Mildred slapped her ear. "Despite the suffering, I must admit, I didn't think I would enjoy this as much as I am."

Ylva grinned, tucking a paintbrush behind her ear. "Ladies, this is Skye. If we let the weather stop us going out, then we'd never go out."

"Spoken like a true Scot."

"But we're with the Scandinavian tour," Mildred pointed out.

"And you'd prefer a man in a kilt wrestling a haggis to the ground for the full Scottish experience?" Ylva asked. She caught a look between the two old ladies. "Don't answer that. Anyway, my mother is Scottish, so I'm not quite as random as you might think."

"But random enough for a selling point," Agnes said. "It was that fact that made your website stand out from the others the tourist board sent us."

"Oh yes," Mildred added. "You reminded me of me when I was young."

Agnes pursed her lips like a wrinkled prune. "Liar."

"Ladies," Ylva interrupted. "No fighting. Perhaps we should get as much sketching done as possible now. I don't like the look of those clouds overhead. We may have to finish these pictures indoors."

Ylva – owner and sole guide of Scandinavian tours on Skye – was a jumble of stereotypes and contradictions. That and the eclectic mix of offers for touring on her website, as well as languages, made her something of an attraction in her own right. She was a typical blonde and yet she was not. In a standard descriptive sense, she was a natural blonde, thick waves of long blonde hair flowing like water. She was half Swedish, on her father's side, which only played to the Swedish stereotype of blue-eyed (her eyes were brown), blonde-haired ABBA-singing girls with a hurdy-gurdy accent and an innocence of the wicked ways of the world. On the other hand, she was quite bright, cynical and ferociously independent. She wasn't known for her singing either. Being half Scottish, on her mother's side, served as a defence when the old Swedish stereotype grew tiresome or people asked her what she thought she was doing living in Scotland. As if people had never moved about since the beginning of human existence.

She had lived on Skye for two years, running her one-man-band touring company of the island. Catering for English and/or Scandinavian speakers (with Swedish she could muddle along with the Norwegians and Danes), she offered tailor made tours of any requested length, from photography and painting, history and archaeology, walking and trekking (but not full blown mountaineering and rock climbing – everyone had their limit) and wildlife and natural history. She'd got herself a name in the tourist circles, both for her odd mix of languages and target groups, and also because she really didn't look like the kind of guide people expected, not quite thirty, driving her paying guests round the mountainous, wild landscape of Skye in her orange VW campervan conversion (from mobile camping home to alternative minibus from the 1960s). There was something about her that screamed eccentric, that and the fact that she was quite happy living alone in a bleak little cottage looking out to sea.

The rain pulled in for the day. Dabbling in watercolours was a pointless exercise even for the more extreme landscape artists. They retreated to a small coffee shop that sold pictures Ylva painted during the winter months. Set up in a conservatory in the back, Mildred and Agnes worked from their sketches and part-finished paintings, with whatever help they required. Ylva drove them back to Portree where they were staying. The ladies wanted an early night as the weather was not good and there was a caelidh planned for later in the week that they wanted to save their energy for. Ylva left them at their Bed and Breakfast.

With an evening suddenly to be longer than expected, she had rung to see if her language meet up could be brought forward, which it couldn't due to a late shift. Sighing, Ylva stuffed her mobile phone back into her bag and went to the supermarket at the edge of the town to stock up before driving home. They had a better choice here than her own little supermarket in the town where she lived.

It grew dark late in the evening at this time of the year, yet with the thick rain clouds hung low and the dark atmosphere, it was as if twilight had been pushed forward by several hours. Ylva switched on the full headlights as she left Portree, climbing up away from the coastal town on the road back around the island bays towards Broadford. She should have really asked Morag if she could have crashed the night, but there had been something inside keen to get home.

Reaching a peak, she could see across the dusky landscape; the road snaking onwards. Car headlights coming in her direction cut through the slashing rain. The vehicle was going at quite a speed and they would meet at a sharp corner. She slowed down, not inclined to be run off the road by some crazy tourist keen to get back to the main town, Portree, and forgetting that these roads needed a little care, especially in wet weather. Approaching the corner, she slowed down and decided to wait. She remembered a few months ago coming upon a nasty accident at this corner. The police were already there, shaking heads at the crushed metal work, the skid marks on tarmac, the doctor searching for a pulse.

Ylva drummed her fingers on the steering wheel in time with the thudding rain. She shivered. This old rust bucket was reliable in that it always started, and with a little attention, worked well with her, but it was persistently cold inside. She wanted to get home.

The song on the radio finished; the next one started.

"Come on," she grumbled to no one. "I want to go home."

The speeding car still didn't make the corner. Leaning against her seatbelt, she stared out of the passenger window, looking for the approaching car. There were no junctions along this stretch of road, so the car had to pass her. Yet she couldn't see it anymore. No blazing headlights; no retreating red rear lights from a vehicle that had changed its mind and turned around to go back the way it had come.

"*Konstigt*," she commented quietly, putting the van into gear and moving forward. Strange. She drove hesitantly around the corner, and the car did not appear. She didn't pass any parked vehicles, and by the time she reached home, she was reasonably convinced that the lights she had seen were a trick of the mind – an illusion from the rain and poor weather, reflecting lights or merely a tired brain toying with her eyes.

"Oh, Il-va!"

Ylva looked up from the passenger seat of her van where she had just set the bag of shopping. Il-va – it sounded like Helena, the woman who worked in Broadford's tourist information office. A lot of people had trouble pronouncing her name; the Swedish y not being a sound happily made by the English language. She'd gotten used to the variety of names she was known by on the island and answered to all kinds of things.

The wind picked up as Helena, dressed in her tourist information officer uniform, neck scarf flapping in the fresh sea breeze like a welcome flag, trotted over the car park. A curious woman, anywhere between mid forties to late sixties, depending on whether you were of the opinion that her looks were due to her age or a past smoking habit now conquered. She'd been working at the Broadford tourist office as long as Ylva had lived here. It was a white wooden shack at one end of the car park, facing a small supermarket servicing the little villages and scatterings of crofts and self-catering cottages speckled uncontrollably across the highland scenery. The car park overlooked Broadford bay on one side; behind mountains pushed up through the horizon.

"Il-va," Helena repeated her name as she reached the tour guide. "I've been looking out for you the last few days. There was a man asking after you the other day."

"A man?"

"From the tourist board."

Ylva wrinkled her brow. "You make it sound like the tourist board has nothing to do with you."

"Ach, no," Helena waved it off. "Only he's from the Scottish tourist board, you know, the central headquarters."

This didn't sound good. She zipped up her jacket as if it would be defence enough against what she was expecting. "Someone's not been making complaints, have they?"

"Oh no, nothing of the sort." Helena paused, giving her a wary look. "Besides, you wouldn't give anyone cause to complain, would you?"

"Well of course not."

"This man is part of their media team, or something of the sort. They're working on new material for the visit Scotland promotions abroad for the next year; television and newspaper adverts and the like. He was telling me they're looking for interesting people working in the industry, a little bit odd…"

"A little bit odd?"

"And I immediately thought of you," Helena continued, ignorant of the look on Ylva's face. "People working in the industry, and the area they work in. Give people a real feel of what they're coming into contact with."

"Sounds like he's really sold you the spiel."

"Oh, I don't know. We just had a wee chat. I've got his details in the office. Come over and you can have them." Helena linked arms with her as if they were conspiratorial schoolgirls plotting about a boy they liked. "You should give him a ring. Won't it be exciting? You'll have your picture in the tourist brochures in a big glossy advert."

"I don't know whether I want to get involved with something like that."

"Of course you do." The woman started walking back to her place of work, dragging Ylva with her. She had a surprising amount of strength, especially factoring in the wind and the point that Ylva was actually the tallest of the pair by a few inches. "Besides, you'll be paid for your time, so you can hardly say no, can you. Ours is not a profitable line of work. And it'll be coverage of your own business as well, won't it now?"

"I suppose." Ylva didn't sound convinced. The door slammed shut as the two women entered the tourist information office. Ylva stood and stared at a spinner of postcards whilst Helena busied herself behind the counter.

"Will you have a cup of tea?"

"No, I've got to be heading up to Portree. I've got clients to meet in an hour."

"Well, I'll just find you that man's number and then I've done what I said I'd do."

Her eyes drifted over the glossy prints of popular scenes of Skye; many taken through coloured filters to show features off to their upmost potential. So many of the views spoke of the vastness, of the wilderness. Two years and still it overwhelmed her sometimes.

"Here we go."

Ylva jumped as Helena reappeared with a yellow post it note in her hand.

"I've got you his email, phone number, mobile phone number…"

"Thanks." She didn't sound too enthusiastic. "Maybe I'll send him an email sometime." She wasn't sure if it was the kind of publicity she needed, being dumped in an advert like a freak show to make people want to come to the island. Skye's real popular, we have Swedes and everything!

"Make it more than a maybe," Helena told her. "There'll be dosh in it for you."

Ylva shoved the note into the back of her wallet as she climbed into the driver's seat. Even Helena's promises of dosh didn't make the offer sound better. There would be something missing in this apparent golden deal, perhaps a misunderstanding between the man and Helena. Besides, she wasn't 100% Scottish – hardly selling the pure Scotland angle.

She drove back up through the island to Portree to pick up Agnes and Mildred from their accommodation. The two ladies were spritely, both with woollen hats pulled down over their ears against the wind. It would die down inland, but wind was always useful for blowing the midges away, and Ylva intended to head out to the coast to take full advantage of the effect.

"Where are we going today?"

"Somewhere midge-free?" Agnes hoped.

"We're going west," Ylva said as she pulled away from the pavement. "We're going west to a place called Neist Point. I think we're going to get some violence in our paintings today."

"Violence? Goodness. What is it they're doing out on Neist Point; fighting?"

"Not as a regular feature, but the sea can be quite rough."

Neist Point, on the west of the island, was a wind-battered jut of tough rock looking out towards the Outer Hebrides. Rugged cliffs, steep hills and a lighthouse planted on the edge, proof against the elements. At the far end, clustered with the lighthouse, pillars of hexagonal-topped rock made their way into the water like uneven, jumbled steps. There was a scattering of hand-build cairns and small towers of rocks, piled up by tourists over the years. The ladies perched like imps, sketchbooks on their knees, drawing the lighthouse. Ylva stood a little way from them, gazing back at the two steep, short hills they had hiked to get down to the lighthouse.

"There was a graveyard here once."

"A graveyard?" Agnes looked up from her sketching. "It seems like a long way to cart anyone's dead body. I suppose it's making an occasion of the moment. What happened; did it wash away into the sea?"

She shook her head. "It wasn't a real graveyard. They set it up for some film – I forget the name – and just didn't bother taking it down afterwards."

Mildred let a laugh loose to the wind. "Ull-vay," she said, "This has been a most curious tour. You are privy to all kinds of strange pieces of information."

She grinned. "My head is full of all kinds of things." She pulled a small ring bound book of watercolour paper from her waterproof jacket pocket. "Now, crowd round and I'll show you a tip for painting sea spray and violent waves."

Ylva was still thinking about that unmanned, automatic lighthouse with its fictional graveyard later that day when she was in the Donart Castle car park. There was something so lonely, so desirably bleak about Neist Point lighthouse as if you might blink, and realise it was as real as the graveyard that was no longer there.

Agnes and Mildred had finished looking around the castle, strolling through the gardens and sketching the loch shore where short boat rides to spot the seals set off. They had opened the van doors, and were laying their sketches and paintings out on the floor for comparison. They looked like a couple of out-of-practice market stall holders trying to flog amateur artwork.

"Now, Ull-vay, you've got to come and judge who's captured the Old Man of Storr best."

She stood behind the two ladies and looked down at their almost matching paintings. A view that had been captured a million times before. "It looks like you've got the local wildlife," she told Mildred, examining the picture a little more closely. "Isn't that a squashed midge in the paint there?"

"Ladies, what is Ylva selling out of the back of her van today?"

They all looked around, a unison of heads snapping in the same direction. Unconsciously Agnes and Mildred adapted that fawning look all the ladies over a certain age got when they saw him. Not yet acquainted with who he was or what he did, yet the response was there, almost animal. It never ceased to amuse Ylva, although she desperately hoped she wouldn't be like this in her later years.

"These are our works of art," Mildred said, already bold with the stranger.

"Looks like you've been having a good stay on Skye."

"We're having a marvellous time. And what about yourself?"

The man, a dark-haired Scot in his thirties, darted his eyes across the paintings and over to Ylva.

"And what are you doing here?"

He laughed. "That's a fine greeting for a friend."

"Ah, whatever," she said. "This is a bit out of your usual area."

"Had a bit of a disaster down at the jetty for the seal boats. A tourist thought they'd broken an ankle disembarking, and I was called out." He paused, as if they were all hanging on his every word. All as a joke. "It was a false alarm."

"So you're a doctor," Mildred said eagerly.

"That I am," he confirmed. "And I will have to be getting back to surgery now. I'll catch you later, Ylva."

"Yeah, later, Dougie."

"Dr Dougie," Mildred whispered to Agnes. They watched as he walked back to his car.

"Do you think we'll be visiting anywhere near the nice young doctor's surgery?"

Ylva smiled wryly. The nice young doctor – she was glad Dougie was out of earshot now. "I doubt it. But considering you've both got such hardy constitutions, it's not something we need concern ourselves with."

"Do you think he'll be at the caelidh you got us tickets for?"

He had worked his trick really quick this time. Ylva pulled open the driver's door. "I have no idea," she told them. Dougie was a nice guy, but his confidence that all old ladies were putty in his hands did not need encouraging. "Let's pack up. There's one more place I want to go before we head back to Portree."

Mildred nudged Agnes later in the minibus when they were on the road. "They'll have medical supervision at the caelidh, they always do," she said as if she was a recognised authority on the matter. "We're going to have a great old time."

"I just know it was those buggers who scarpered early this morning." The man kicked more sand at the scorched patch of ashes. His face wrinkled up even more in disgust. He looked old at the best of times; a lot more than his forty-seven years; his face full of wrinkles as if his skull was too small for his face. Weather-beaten; mapped with experience. He looked over at Ylva, who stood watching, bemused, hands stuffed in her jeans pockets.

"Disgusting."

She looked down at the charred remains. Leftovers of a beach fire on the shore of Loch Brittle on the west coast of the island. The campsite was on the shore, and people had campfires. Colm had worked here several seasons and knew how things went. "I don't understand. Did they throw their meat in the bonfire?"

Colm looked unimpressed. He was incapable of hiding his irritation with anyone's idiocy; even momentary lapses. Picking up a blackened stick, he poked at the central contortion as if about to start a lecture. "It's a cat."

"A cat?"

"Roasted."

"But who would want to eat a cat?"

"Ylvay, they didn't throw the cat in the fire for dinner. It was torture." He tapped protrusions on the body. "Look at the way the wee paws are tied together."

"You're not suggesting it was alive when it went on the fire?"

"Drugged up, I bet. Bloody sickos." He raised his eyes and met Ylva's stare. They both knew his youth had been an exploratory journey into the world of narcotics. "I never went in for shite like this."

"Are you going to call the police?"

"I don't know." Colm tossed the stick back on the extinguished bonfire. "The buggers won't even be on the island anymore. I don't suppose the police'll be much bothered."

"But you should report it. They'll want to keep an eye on stuff like this."

"Aye." Colm stuffed his hands in his pockets and turned away. "Call out the crime squad. There's been a *murr-da*." He exaggerated the statement, playing up his Dundee accent.

Ylva followed him back into the campsite. There were a few tents and a couple of mobile homes parked up, but the season was only just getting going. In the height of summer the site would be humming, people slapping themselves in a primitive beat as the midges got too much, climbing up to the Cullin Mountains for a better view and fewer insects.

The campsite on the inlet's shores, at the base of Glen Brittle, was a prime location with the rocky mountains rising up from the ground beyond like a surrounding boundary fence. This bay was the starting point for many walks and treks up into the mountains. Most didn't properly get to the top of the mountains, - being particularly rocky and dangerous, they were perfect for climbers and people training for adventures such as the Himalayas. Ylva walked and she hiked, but she had never caught the rock climbing bug and had never been to the top. She'd sat in a moorland basin at the very foot of the mountains further up the glen once when Colm and some friends had climbed the waterpipe – a challenging vertical gully in a triangular peak called *Sgurr an Fheadain*. Ylva finished her book and got a lot of sketching and painting down. It took the climbers about seven hours to get up the shaft.

"Take a wee stroll up to the cairn?"

"Maybe not as far as the cairn, but a bit of the way," Ylva answered, looking up to the mountains. It would take heading on three hours if they went all the way up to the cairn, and she hadn't really wanted to do anything strenuous this evening.

They walked past the campsite buildings, over a stile and started on the path upwards away from sea-level. Colm led the way. A wiry, sinew stretched man; he wasn't much to look at, but his stamina was yet to be beaten.

"How's business treating you?"

"All right. I've got a few booked in for the coming months. Just took a couple of old ladies back to the mainland today. I've had a good week with them."

"That's the life, working in the tourist industry. Like you're always on holiday," he joked.

"Are you going to be working at the camp site this summer again?"

"Aye, most likely."

Colm usually helped out most summers at the campsite. He did some occasional rock-climbing tours into the Cullins and was also a member of the mountain rescue team. Beyond that, Ylva didn't really know what he did with himself, other than walking and climbing. She didn't know how he survived financially, because he couldn't earn that much from any of his haphazard occupations. But he kept his small home near Sligachan, and lived relatively comfortably.

Perhaps it was a fortune he had saved in his youth. He had worked incredibly hard when he had been in the forestry industry in Sweden. He'd gone over with one of her mother's cousins and stayed with the family in Umeå – a town in the northern half of Sweden – for a couple of weeks whilst setting themselves up with work and somewhere to live. The cousin hadn't lasted long, not caring for the physical work nor trying to get away with the language, but something about all that fresh air and wilderness had sucked Colm right in, and he had stayed for almost eight years. He'd then gone up north and over the top to work in Finland, before eventually returning to Scotland. He'd been living in Skye for a couple of years by the time Ylva had moved to the island to start a new life, although she hadn't known at the time. It had only been when she'd taken a group down through Glen Brittle to the loch, that she'd bumped into him at the camp site, and recognised him from her adolescence days.

They climbed up a steep section of path, and stopped to look back at the coastline from their higher vantage point.

"*Fan. Jävligt vackert,*" Colm commented, switching to Swedish. Damn it. Bloody beautiful. He was fluent, but his passive language was better than his active, and he had always kept that stilted Scottish accent to his Swedish, which got stronger as the years away from the country and regular practice grew.

Ylva laughed out loud. It was a running joke. "*Allt jag hör från dig är svördommar numera.*" All I ever hear from you is swearing these days. "I bet that's all you remember of your Finnish."

He put a roll-up cigarette between his thin lips. "*Satans Perkele.*"

She laughed again. "I rest my case."

"Finnish was a damn hard language. I spent all my time with loggers and all I did learn was swearing. I was very proficient, but I couldn't have a polite conversation with the boss. I'm telling you, that's why I got fired."

"A likely story."

"How's the Gaelic going then?"

"It's coming along."

He smiled wryly to himself. "I could never be bothered myself, and I'm Scottish."

"So am I."

Colm ignored her comment. "I've never been one for learning languages for the hell of it, mind you; and everyone here speaks English. I got away with the Swedish over there, but my spelling and grammar was crap. And you Swedes are so good at your English. One of my bosses used to tell me to write my reports in English. I remember getting really mad at him; telling him I could speak bloody *svenska*. He said he wanted to practise his English." Colm sucked on the cigarette. "Lazy Scandinavian git. He couldn't be doing with deciphering my written Swedish no more."

"I thought that was just your writing in general."

He waggled his finger. "And that's the Scandinavian sense of humour. It's not funny."

"Unlike your writing."

"No need to be unfriendly, abusing my writing."

"You were abusing my countrymen."

"I thought you said you were Scottish."

She shrugged and turned back the way they had come. "I have the best of both worlds. Shall we head back? I'm not feeling so overly energetic for walking this evening."

"Aye." Colm stubbed out his cigarette. "We'll go have a few bevies and put the world to rights."

Ylva wasn't as good at languages as she might have been. She was fluent in Swedish and English, which could have sounded impressive, only that she had been brought up bilingual. Under those circumstances no particular effort was required for learning either. The fact was, so they said, that children of bilingual upbringing were more adapt at learning more languages. The brain was more capable of thinking in different ways, speaking with different tongues. Ylva wasn't fluently multilingual beyond her parental tongues. She'd studied French and Russian at school, got along reasonably well, but lack of use since coming out of the educational system had seen the foreign languages quickly waste away.

She was now trying to learn Gaelic, and was coming along quite well comparatively speaking in that she had been doing this for a year and a half and was still trying. But the grammar was hard and the gap between the written word and pronunciation was vast. Russian had been more awkward in some ways, but the very fact that she instinctively knew the letters used for the Gaelic alphabet muddled her brain when it turned out they were always pronounced the way she would have thought impossible. At least Russian was written with a completely different alphabet.

It had been lonely first moving to Skye. Wanting to soak up everything about island life she could, she had put an advert on a community websites, stating that she wanted to learn Gaelic. She couldn't afford to spend money on lessons, so had suggested one-to-one tuition instead, on the basis of language exchange. You teach me Gaelic and I'll teach you Swedish. Not an obviously large market.

She'd had two replies, and in the end it was not a native of Skye, but of Lewis, now resettled, who had endured. The other, a Portree local called Morag, had been pleasant company but had no interest in learning languages and was a poor, disinterested teacher. They got along well enough, and were friends now, sticking to the common ground of English.

Ylva checked her watch as she hurried down the road to the pub. She was in Portree for their arranged language exchange and she was already quarter of an hour late. Not that it mattered, after a year and a half the arrangement had become very informal and flexible.

Pushing open the door, she stepped into the pub. Small, low-ceiling rooms, an open fire, beams ingrained with the distant scent of wood smoke. There were a few people in, low conversations. There was supposed to be a band playing later on in the evening.

She stepped into the main room, stretching her neck a little to look over the collection of people. Across at the back of the room, by the window, sat the doctor with a pint glass. Dr Douglas MacWhirter. Dark, wavy hair just slightly longer than you might expect of a regular doctor, which always gave him a look that he'd just stumbled off a fishing boat (what he had been doing on the boat she could never work out, but in her mind it was often a Norwegian trawler boat for some indecipherable reason). He raised his hand to her.

"*Ciamar a tha thu?*"

Ylva walked over to the table. Shrugging off her shoulder bag, the strap crossing diagonally over her body, she dropped it into the window seat before setting herself in the empty chair. "Dougie," she greeted him. She was still uncomfortable speaking a lot of Gaelic, and despite the fact that this was a language exchange at her own suggestion, she would avoid the work as much as possible. "I'm all right."

He broke out into a wide smile, chuckling. "*Ciamar a tha thu?*" He repeated. How are you?

"Ah, come off it. We don't need to start straight away."

"*Ciamar a tha thu?*"

Ylva scowled at him. "*Chan eil dona, tapadh leat.*" Not bad, thanks.

He lent back in his chair and clapped lightly. "Hey, you can remember something."

"One or two words. *Som om du är redo för att samtala på svenska med mig.*" As if you're ready for talking in Swedish with me.

"Sorry, didn't quite catch your muttering there." Dougie took a drink from his pint. "*Jag lärar mig svenska.*"

"*Du lär dig.*"

"Sorry?"

"*Du lär dig.*" You're learning. "You don't need the –ar there."

"Oh, right, aye." He considered her for a moment. "Well, this has been a fine howdy-do to start off this evening. Shall we start over without the aggression?"

Ylva grinned. "There's nothing aggressive about me. Besides, you started it."

"I only asked you how it's going," he scoffed, pretending to be offended. "Now, Ylva, are you not having anything to drink?"

She paused, thinking over some of the phrases she'd read in the book she'd been flicking through the other evening. After a year and a half she ought to be able to say something. "*Bu toigh leam cupan tì an-dràsda.*" I'd like a cup of tea just now.

"A whole sentence. Wow, I'm impressed. How long did it take you to memorise that?"

"Oh sod off, Dougie," Ylva said as she stood up.

"I'm only joking."

She gave him a strange look. For a moment he'd looked as though he actually thought she was taking him seriously, getting offended. "I'm going to the bar," she said. "I'll be back in a minute."

Whilst she was waiting at the bar for her pot of tea, one of the older locals nudged her in the side of the arm. Ylva looked across, recognising the saggy, wrinkled face and white hair. "Hamish," she nodded to him. "Propping up the bar again?"

"Ach, no, not propping exactly. Just one drink before I'm away home. I see you and your doctor are here again. Having your lessons are you?"

"Something like that." She passed money over the bar to pay for the tea.

"I see he's giving you a bit of stick."

"I know," she sighed melodramatically. "It's very trying, you know."

"I'll teach you a word," Hamish said. "You say this next time he starts on you. *Muc sheòbhaineach fhireann*. All the young lassies are saying it these days to the lads. Seems to be a popular thing."

Ylva smiled, having no idea what he was talking about. "Say it again."

"*Muc sheòbhaineach fhireann*."

"*Muc...*"

"*Muc sheòbhaineach fhireann*."

"*Muc sheòbhaineach fhireann*." She repeated, a little unsteady with the unfamiliar words. "All right, got it. I'll use it next time."

"You do that."

Dougie couldn't keep himself from asking straight off when Ylva returned to their table. She was bent over, setting the tea tray on the corner, taking the teapot off. "What was Hamish saying to you?"

"Hamish?" She glanced up at him. "Just giving me a few words of advice."

"Advice? What kind of advice. Do you think it's wise taking advice off a man in a pub?"

She sat down again. "He merely said the next time you start bothering me, I was to say *Muc sheòbhaineach fhireann* to you."

Dougie burst out laughing. "Now that, I am not. I'm sure I'm not." He paused, leaning closer in. "You don't really think so?"

"I haven't the slightest idea what it means."

"Male chauvinistic pig."

"Oh." She sat up straight, a little surprised that Hamish would have come out with something like that. "Well, I don't know." She took her notebook out of her bag and opened it up. Pushing it across the table to Dougie, she said: "Why don't you write it down for me and I'll think about it."

They chatted in the pub until the band came on, sometimes stumbling through a bit of Gaelic and a few words of Swedish. They discussed expressions of colour in depth, and Ylva wrote down a list of all the colours in Gaelic, having forgotten that they had already taken this word collection several months ago. The pub filled up, a mix of tourists to sample local music; the locals wanting a night out, warm and cosy, marinated in good music.

The band, a trio, looked as though they were barely out of their teens. Age wasn't any comment on their talent – they must have been born playing musical instruments. Music was a spirit kept alive on the islands, entwined with the pub and caelidh cultures. The only girl in the group played an electric violin – a solitary nod to modern times, the two lads playing the guitar and small pipes respectively. The piper had vividly dyed red hair, cut in a mothball effect with no obvious pattern, merely patches of closely shorn hair, patches of long flops that caught the light as he nodded his head to the beat of the music. Sometimes he sang – he was the only one who dared take his voice to the microphone – sometimes they played jigs and reels. The last song before their break had lyrics, a fast upbeat traditional folk song, with their own arrangements weaved in. It was hard to follow the full gist of the lyrics, but unexpected words for a song would leap out. Ylva was intrigued.

When the song finished and the band announced the break, Ylva looked over at Dougie. He seemed to be away with the fairies; she leant forward and tapped his hand, catching his attention. "I'm just going to speak to the band."

He raised his eyebrows. "They're a bit young for you, aren't they?"

Ylva rolled her eyes as she got up from the table. "I want to know what that song is."

She passed by groups of people, queues for the bar, lost looking souls searching out the toilets. Past by the "stage-area" – a glorified description of an alcove with a couple of amplifiers, and to the corner of the bar. The girl and one of the boys had disappeared. The piper with the red hair was taking a slug out of a water bottle. He put it down on the bar and moved to pull his sweater off when he noticed Ylva. He paused, flashing her a grin. "Did you like the gig?"

"Sure. I was wanting to ask you something."

"Sure, no problem. This your first time to Skye?"

Oh, he thinks I'm a tourist, Ylva realised as she pulled her notepad out of her bag, flicking through to a blank page. It was at times like this she wished she spoke better Gaelic than she did. "I live here," she told him, trying to keep the irritation out of her voice.

"Really?" he perked up at this. "I've no' seen you about."

She caught the look in his eye and felt her age. She must have had at least ten years on this boy. "I run a tour company," she explained. A tour company – it sounded like a proper business with employees and stationary rather than the scruffy old converted camper van and her home-made website. "I'm always kind of researching the island. You know, more information for the tours. That last song you sang…"

"That's not a song from Skye," he quickly told her. "It's just a traditional song. In fact, I think it might be English." He wrinkled his nose.

"Oh, right," she faltered a little. She hadn't really wanted to know for the tours, if she was honest; only that there was something about the song that was sticking on to her immediate focus. She wanted to know more. "Could you write down the lyrics for me?"

"The lyrics?" He looked from the offered notepad and pen, to Ylva as if she was mad.

Behind him a door opened and the girl peered into the bar. "Chris," she called over to him. "Are you coming out for a ciggie or not?"

"Sure." He turned back to Ylva. "I haven't really got the time right now."

"What about the title? I could search for it."

"You really are keen, aren't you?" he said, taking the pad as if he were about to write an autograph for her. "Look, this is my email. Drop me a line and I'll send you the lyrics when I've got a free moment."

The busy life of the teenager. He passed the book to her and went to his friends. Ylva looked down at the notepad. She felt like an idiot, and an aging one at that. Why did she even need to have this song so desperately? It didn't matter. She looked back across the bar and saw Dougie wave at her, having seen the whole exchange with the sound turned off. He'd be teasing her about this for weeks to come.

People said – who 'people' were, she wasn't sure, but it was a well-known fact – that people (presumably people other than the people who were saying this in the first place) either loved or hated Skye. There was no in between. Ylva was well-acquainted with the rumour, but she had never seen it manifest quite so quickly and venomously as it was today.

"I know you're supposed to be into all this tourist-shit," the woman said as she took a packet of slim cigarettes from her bag. "And be all amazed by the scenery or something, but I am really not a tourist." She lit the cigarette, inhaled once, then held it down by her side between two fingers as if she could no longer be bothered. "This is such a bleak place. It feels dead." And with that final conclusion, she made her way back to the mini bus.

This was a Skye-in-a-day tour. It was something Ylva was not particularly keen on or advertised, but the customer was always right, and she could hardly turn away business. Day tours could be good, if focused on one aspect or area. But to expect to "do" an island in a day missed the point for Ylva. How could you do justice to an island under such time limitations?

The American family she was escorting – mother, father, son, daughter – were "doing" Great Britain in two weeks. The father was enthusiastic to the point of having a fit (he had Scottish roots); the mother had made it quite clear what she thought of Skye and tourism in general; the teenage son said nothing and the teenage daughter didn't seem to be quite all there. The father embodied what most people expected of American tourists in Scotland. Ylva had taken several Americans round Skye and at times, the stereotypes were spot on; likewise they were utterly irrelevant on other occasions. Every country had its share of personalities.

Having given almost an entire week of their schedule over to "doing" Scotland, they were spending a day on Skye, expecting to see and experience the entire island, before catching the ferry at Uig across the waves to Tarbert on Harris – one of the outer Hebridian islands. Ylva had picked them up from the station at Kyle of Lochalsh on the mainland early that morning. They'd come from Inverness, having "done" the Highlands, and ready to move on to the islands. Father was already enthusing; mother was scowling. Ylva had assumed the woman was just tired, but she was realising that mother was one of these people who were rarely, if ever, happy.

They had sounded so keen in the emails. It was a miserable climax to the enthusiastic planning, and now there was an entire day of rushing through the sights with this family to get through. The father had been enthusiastic; he still was – hurrying up and down the river bank taking photographs of the Cullins as if they were in imminent danger of collapsing. They were at Sligachan, at the feet of the Cullin Mountains and a stunning, iconic view of Skye. The river, a shallow mountain stream spread out, cut through the earth, scatterings of reddy-brown tinged rocks and boulders strewn across. There was a stone arched bridge a little way up from the main road bridge. The teenage son stood at one end of the bridge, large headphones set on his head, his body shrugged back into a baggy hooded sweater. The daughter looked like a hippy who didn't really know what was going on; perched on one of the larger rocks on the side of the shallow river. She was gazing into the water, perhaps at her own reflection; her feathery blonde hair dipping into the upland-chill.

"This sure is a stunning view." Enthusiastic father popped up beside Ylva on the middle of the bridge. "Good call. I've got some great shots." He clutched at his expensive digital camera.

Ylva looked over at him. A greying man in his fifties. Stocky and dumpy were words that could describe him, but gave a false impression of his height, for he was certainly six foot tall, if not a little more. A moustache like a broom bristled out from under his nose. She smiled politely. "I always like to bring visitors here."

"So, Ull-ba," the father continued. "Now we've seen Scottish water, will we be going on to sample the real water of life?"

Oh lord, Ylva thought, they should put you on a bus with a microphone.

His eyebrows dropped a little in concern when she didn't immediately answer. "There is a distillery on Skye…"

They had discussed this at length by email when they had booked the day tour. Whisky seemed to be an obligatory part of experiencing Scotland – at least the tourists thought so. "Of course, Tallisker," she assured him. "We're on our way there. We have to drive right past this view, so I thought it was worth a five minute stop."

"Sure was."

"Ok, folks," Ylva raised her voice so the teenagers would hear. The daughter looked up from the water; the son shrugged his shoulders slightly to signal he was listening. "Let's get back to the minibus. Next stop Tallisker."

It was proving to be a long day. Ylva pulled on the handbrake and switched off the engine. Donart Castle car park again. It had been under more mutually pleasant circumstances when last here, with Agnes and Mildred. This time it was only a day tour and it felt as though she'd been stuck with this family for a fortnight already.

They'd done the obligatory whisky distillery tour. Gauging some of the mother's comments, this wasn't the first distillery tour since they'd arrived in Scotland. The guide had arrived to take the visitors. Ylva remained in the bar, a first floor view out onto the waterfront at the bottom end of the village Carbost, where the distillery was. Here they were essentially level with the water, but the village was on a steep incline down grassy slopes rolling towards this little bay and in one sense or more the distillery. Across the water the island continued, this patch a sea inlet. The woman looking after the ten-year-old they measured out in small amounts as a sampler to the tourists, came over and offered Ylva a drink. She'd unfortunately had to decline – drinking whilst driving clients was hardly the way to ensure a good reputation and stars from the tourist board.

"So what have you brought us to now?"

The mother's words snapped her out of her reflections. Ylva looked up sharply from the windscreen to the trees that surrounded the car park. This was a curious part of Skye, cultivated with a thick covering of trees – quite different from most of the open upland nature of the island. "This is Donart Castle," she answered.

"Certainly looks like a tourist trap," mother commented, casting an eye over the number of parking spaces.

"Is this an old ruin?" The father gazed eagerly out of the window as if expecting to see turrets looming over the top of the trees.

"No. This is still lived in. It's a family home. One of the main families on Skye, historically speaking."

Ylva crossed over the road to the entrance to the castle grounds, the family loitering behind. There was a green wooden shed with hatch where the tickets were sold, along with the usual array of brochures in major languages, including the Swedish edition Ylva had translated, postcards and other paraphernalia.

"Eelva!" the dark-haired woman at the ticket booth greeted her. "You got another group for us?"

"Yep, a family." She tried to look more enthusiastic than she felt. Stepping up to the hatch, she rested an arm against the desk and peered in at Maired. A forty-something mother who sold tickets part time and had moved here because of the husband about ten years ago. A pleasant enough woman. Ylva had never seen her outside of the ticket hutch, and found it hard to imagine her having legs.

Ylva fumbled with her purse, taking out her discount card.

"Ach, you don't need to get that out, I know you've got it." Maired tapped a few numbers into the till.

"So how's life treating you these days?"

"Well enough," Maired nodded, watching the paper tickets print off. "Did you know I'm going to be a model?"

Ylva shot her a look. "A model?"

"Oh aye, for the tourist board." Maired grinned. "They're wanting to use people who work in the industry. Come to think of it, you'll know about it. Your name was mentioned. Well, not your name exactly, but he mentioned a Scandinavian tour guide, and you're the only one I can think of." She laughed – the sound an unconscious trademark she threw in on the end of a lot of statements, whether they were funny or not.

"I don't really know about this," Ylva started. "Helena mentioned something about it. I'm supposed to email."

"Oh, you want to get on and get in touch before he changes his mind," the woman assured her. "We'll get paid you know, even if they don't decide to use our shots.

Although I must admit, it'll be quite odd if we are finding our pictures in all the brochures for next year."

"I don't suppose we'd see most of them," Ylva said as she took her change. "Most of it will be used abroad."

"I suppose you're right. It'll still be a bit of fun, though."

Donart castle, situated in well-groomed gardens, was perhaps not the most dramatic looking of Scottish castles from the outside. It had a fine vantage point, built on an outcrop of rock, looking down onto rocky shores of the sea loch, low-tide rocks in the water where seals would bask, and further beyond on the other side of the water, flat-topped hills served as a backdrop. The castle had been the family home and seat of the clan for hundreds of years and was still lived in. It was a little surreal that it was a home as well as a tourist attraction. How was one supposed to relax when the tourists had gone home but the information boards still hung on the walls, the ropes still marking the route people should take through the building.

On the bridge up to the main doors of the castle, Ylva handed guidebooks – her own copies for use on the tours – to each family member; the mother handing her copy straight back. "This is Donart Castle, the ancestral home of the McDuff family," Ylva started as she put the mother's unwanted guide back into her satchel. "I suggest you go through the castle first, then take a look around the gardens. It's worth walking down to the sea front, where you can get some good views of the castle. They do boat tours out from the jetty to go out and watch the seals, but I'm afraid with our itinerary, we're not going to have time for that..."

The corners of the daughter's mouth turned down to an almost cartoon grimace; the mother whispered 'thank god' under her breath.

Ylva couldn't face giving them a tour around the castle. "I suggest you all go at your own pace. If you have any questions, there are people in the rooms you can ask, you've got your guide books..." except Grumpy "and you can come and ask me – I'll be around. I suggest we meet back at the minibus at quarter to four. Does that sound okay with everyone?"

"Marvellous," the mother said sarcastically, flouncing into the shade of the castle. Her humour had not been improving with the day.

The father raised his camera. "Do you know if we can take pictures inside?"

Ylva shook her head. "Sorry, no photography indoors."

The remaining four entered the building, and soon dispersed, gladly mixing with the collection of visitors as if finally relieved that they did not all have to be together. Ylva ambled along behind, soon losing sight of her wards. Nodding hello to the room stewards she knew, she headed upstairs into the banquet hall.

She stood in front of the fairy flag, a smallish flag pinned up in a glass case on the wall. The flag was of undetermined age and source – although there were various stories to explain its history – a grubby brown from age, embroidery that was now hard to follow.

The teenage daughter joined her by the case. "That doesn't look like much."

"The fairy flag?"

"Fairy flag?" the girl's eyes widened as if she had never heard of such a thing. "You're not joking me?"

Ylva idly pointed at the information card stood on the table below.

"Really, that is so cool," the daughter declared. "I'd heard about fairies over here, but we haven't really seen anything..." she drifted off for a moment, gazing up at the flag, and Ylva wondered if the girl was talking about evidence of folklore or the little people themselves.

"I mean, do people still believe in fairies here?"

She shrugged. "Some do, to a point. I don't suppose it's as openly admitted to as it once was. But there must be some superstition alive. There are still offerings left..."

"You guys leave offerings to the fairies?" She clasped her hands together. Ylva was a little taken aback; this was the most active response she'd had from the girl all day. It was turning into a cliché – clap if you believe in fairies – but she didn't suppose it was easy to be of this turn of mind with a mother like that.

"There's a few places on the island where people still leave offerings."

"But nowhere on the itinerary."

"Well, no, but…" Her gaze drifted from the girl staring wistfully at the flag to the bored mother in the background looking out of the window to the sunlight. She could hear the father, not see him, questioning one of the room stewards. The itinerary had been planned from the father's emails. "But maybe we can make an addition to the route."

The girl didn't seem to hear her. "So this flag, do you, like, wave it to summon the fairies?"

"Not exactly. It's supposed to bring guaranteed victory to the clan if they take it into battle with them; but only for a certain number of times. I think it's just the one more chance they've got with it. Kind of like the genie in the lamp with the three wishes."

"And where did it come from?"

"Oh, there's all sorts of stories, versions of the legends. I suppose the reality is long forgotten now." Ylva paused, peering at the time-worn embroidery still clinging to parts of the small flag. "I think my favourite version is that it was a blanket from the son of one of the heads of the family many years ago. It was said that he married a fairy."

The girl gazed lovingly at the flag. "I wish I could meet the fairies," she sighed.

Ylva raised an eyebrow. "Of course, there are other island tales of the fairies being nasty little beasts that live in the woodlands, so it's all dependant on your perspective really. But they have a good bookshop here if you're wanting to read about the folklore of the island."

The girl soon drifted away from her. Ylva made her way through the corridors and rooms, a route she was all too familiar with, having shown countless parties the highlights of the island. Footsteps tapping down the staircase, she arrived in the lower level of the castle, where the kitchens and stores originally would have been. It was a whitewashed corridor with small windows high in the wall lighting the passage. Off to her left there was a row of small rooms with various exhibitions and the all-important bookshop. Along the wall between the open doorways, was a collection of large black and white photographs, mostly taken on the island of St Kilda.

Ylva always slowed down when she reached these pictures, caught by the stony gaze of the wind-hardened people; beefy women whose bodies had adapted to endurance; bearded grizzled men. St Kilda, out in the Atlantic, was a rocky, rough collection of little islands, no longer inhabited. When there had been a community, the people had been the tenants of the chief of Donart Castle. It was said that when the chief died, the cuckoos flew over to St Kilda to let the tenants know. Otherwise the birds would not go to the island.

She followed the line of pictures to the end, where she found an image she could not recall. Checked the title; Uig – a little town on northern Skye, where the ferries across to the Outer Hebrides set off. This was an older photograph from the 1800s; a crofting family outside their cottage. Stony, suspicious gazes examined the photographer, as he captured their image for posterity. A dog paused in the corner, enough sense to stay still long enough to become part of the image. An old woman who was probably not even forty, shawl pulled over her wind-tattered hair. A younger woman with a lined face, holding a baby; a couple of toddlers at her feet. And a young woman, barely twenty if that, with glossy curls and a particularly melancholic stare. She was caught up in the muddle of the family and yet looked out of place. She didn't belong there, or at least her mind was somewhere else.

"I hope we're not giving you the wrong impression."

Ylva involuntarily jumped. Scattering from the photograph, she was surprised to find the son in such close proximity. Not only that, but he had a voice. His headphones were around his neck. Eyes searching.

"Excuse me?"

"About Americans."

"Americans?" Ylva didn't immediately follow his train of thought.

"I hope you're not going to prejudge all Americans on us. My mother is…" he paused, searching for the right word. "Frustrated."

She smiled reassuringly. "I hardly think four people would be a suitably sized representation to base an opinion of a country on. Besides, I've taken all kinds of nationalities around – you get all kinds of people from all kinds of countries."

"But you must pick up on national traits."

"Ah, ah, and if I do, that's my secret," she told him. "And in defence of your mother, going round looking at old ruins and scenery isn't everyone's cup of tea."

"Everyone's cup of tea," he repeated quietly, enjoying the phrase.

"People do say that you either hate or love Skye. There's no in between."

"What about the whole of Scotland?"

She smiled and looked at the ground. "I'm guessing this was exclusively your father's idea; to come to Scotland."

"Yeah, he's finding himself. But hey, we got a free trip to Europe."

"And what do you think about it?"

"What, Europe?"

"In your own words of ten or less," Ylva joked. "I was meaning Skye to be specific."

"I don't know," he started as they walked down the corridor and out of the castle. "I haven't made my mind up. But I doubt if a day is long enough to really experience this place. Or anywhere. I'm not so crazy about all this rushing around; you know, that we have to *do* everything as quickly as possible. I'd like to slow down. But we've got an itinerary to keep and Dad has to be back at the office in a week." He paused, looking over at Ylva. "I don't mean any offence to you. I mean, this is your business."

"This is a busy day – the island in a day? Believe it or not, I do run some more laid back tours."

"You have such a cool job," he decided. "Are you just doing this for a couple of years before going back to where you come from? Where was that; Sweden?"

She felt uncomfortable, quite abruptly. Ylva looked over to the sea, the rocky coastline. "I can't say I've really planned that far ahead."

"Well, I want to do something like that when I finish college." He looked back at the castle. "You know you've filled my sister's head with fairies, right? She's expecting to go and pray to them or something before we get the ship out of here."

"Don't worry about it. I've got it covered."

Ylva was convinced she had seen someone standing on top of the hill. A figure, blurred and silhouetted against the angle of the sun, caught by the corner of her eye. When she looked back again, her view shaded by hand to brow, there was no one there, the top of the hill flat and featureless.

"So this is what again? A fairy glen?"

"It certainly is," the daughter breathed to her father. "I can feel it."

They were stood in a lush, grassy valley between two steep hills, aggressively close to one another. Everything was in miniature, as if man-made. Hills the size of two or three storey houses, collected together in this one patch of the island. Lumps and bumps as if the land had been bitten by a plague of midges. Strange valleys snaking through the meeting place, to the small pond by which the single-track road cut through the area. Ylva had parked the mini bus here. They'd left the mother on a wooden bench by the pond, smoking yet another cigarette in a haughty, off-hand manner, and walked into the fairy glen.

"I don't remember reading about this in the guide books," the father said.

"Oh look, a cave!" the daughter pointed up the side of a steep bank. At the top rocky edges burst out of the earth, hanging over the mouth of a small cave, tree roots gnarling round the corner. Small offerings dangled from the roots, cutting up the otherwise black canvas of the entrance. "I have to leave something."

The son rolled his eyes, hovering for a moment to watch his sister scramble up the slope. He shrugged back into his sweater and sauntered off up the valley.

Ylva looked over at the father. "This isn't really such a publicised place; although there isn't any particular reason for that," she quickly added. "I find the land formations here quite interesting, and it does have its connection back to old folklore."

"Fairies?" the man raised his eyebrows. As if she were taking him for a fool.

"Fairies are a big part of Scottish folklore," Ylva told him. "The belief still exists in some form. People do actually leave offerings here – although I think increasingly it's more for the novelty rather than any particular belief."

Further up the valley, the land opened out as the hills backed off from one another. In this plain a number of shapes – spirals and lovehearts – had been marked out in the grass with fist-sized rocks. Offerings had been cast into the centres, everything scrappy and precious, found in a pocket or lying somewhere in the glen itself, or brought specially for the occasion. Mostly small coins from around the world, hair grips and bobbles, small animal bones and feathers. Even small pieces of jewellery.

The father walked on, intending to circle back to the minibus quickly. He was growing restless, ready to return to Uig to catch the ferry. He felt he had done Skye: the famous view from the bridge, the whisky, the castle and up north to take a quick look at the Quiraing. It was time to move on to Harris.

Ylva crouched down by the side of a small rock-lined circle. This one hadn't been as frequented as some of the larger and more elaborate designs, and picking for the fairies were meagre here. She grubbed through her jacket pocket and pulled out a twenty-pence piece, dropping it into the circle. Something for the entrance fee.

They were at the fairy glen twenty minutes at most before the family were complaining they wanted to get back to the small ferry terminal. Ylva marched back into the hills to fetch the daughter who seemed to be knelt praying in the centre of the spiral. When told they needed to leave now, she'd walked back out following the coiled pathway.

The rain had started on the return drive along the narrow, single-tracked route back down past the farm and steep banks towards the coast and Uig. Pelting on the roof. Inside there was an uncomfortable silence. Everyone was ready for the ferry for different reasons.

Parking at the seafront, the mother and children were quickly out of the vehicle and into the small ferry terminal building. The girl had smiled at Ylva on the way past, the son nodded and the mother said nothing. Ylva pulled her jacket hood over her head and went to help the father drag the heavy cases across to the building for the next stage of their journey. They shook hands in the entrance, making polite thanks and comments before separating.

Ylva returned to the bus in the thrashing rain. Droplets drumming against her waterproof jacket, turning into small rivers that ran across her head and dripped down from the edge of the hood. Hair that poked out from the collar was saturated quickly. She slung herself into the driver's seat and shut the door, scattering raindrops across the inside of the windscreen. That had been a long day. Thank god it was over.

The sun pulled out from the clouds, immediate warmth to the air. The rain continued heavily, but the atmosphere seemed to brighten. Ylva smiled as she backed out of the parking space. She had an entire day to herself tomorrow and she was going walking.

Turning onto the main road south, it pulled up away from Uig and the coast and back into the hills. Ahead on the left hand side, a rather pathetic and bedraggled figure stood in the gravel. Drenched clothes hung shapelessly around the woman's body, her hair in rats' tails. As Ylva drove nearer, she saw the woman was holding a pair of shoes in one hand, as if she'd just come from the beach and was waiting for her feet to dry. It would be a long wait in this weather.

"*Jävlar*," Ylva muttered under her breath. Bloody hell. She drove past the woman, slowing the van down and indicating left. She wasn't in the habit of picking up hitchhikers, but the woman had looked so forlorn and rain-sodden, it seemed inhuman to drive past.

She pulled on the handbrake and put the vehicle in neutral. Drummed her fingers on the steering wheel and watched the steady beat of the windscreen wipers, clearing another torrent of water. The woman didn't come.

Maybe she didn't understand that Ylva was offering her a lift. She twisted in her seat, pulling against the seatbelt but the back window had steamed up. It was difficult to see much in her droplet-sodden side mirrors. She touched the car horn, jumping by how loud it was. Waited a minute. No one came.

Opening the door, Ylva stepped out into the rain. Walked the length of her van. The woman wasn't where she had been. She could have started walking, of course, but looking one way then the other, Ylva couldn't see anyone on the road, and a pedestrian couldn't have walked out of sight that quickly, surely.

She wiped the rainwater from her eyes, making a full tour around her mini-bus. She was definitely the only person wandering in the rain on the main road that afternoon.

Five long years I waited with no news. Every day I sat by the window with the view to the path and watched. I saw the weather and the seasons go over our beautiful land. And you did not appear.

I helped my mother carding the wool. Baking the bread. Lighting the fire and cleaning our cottage. Working in the fields; listening to the men gossip and pretending that I did not notice when they talked about you. For it was a great secret, even from you. It still is from the others.

I like to think, that had you known, you would have come back, hurrying down that path to the village. Eager to see my smile. But I know it would not have happened like that. I would have to go to you, as I do now as I creep out of my parent's croft and start up the hills and away from the sea that has watched over me and been my view since the day I was born. But I have heard tell that you are back on the island, further south of here. And I should remain; I should wait, perhaps for an eternity. But I cannot help myself. I am coming.

Ylva was humming the tune to the song she neither knew the title nor words to as she walked down the bank. Hooked her fingers under the straps of her rucksack and continued warbling. She hoped she would get a reply to her question.

It was a day off – something that became increasingly irregular as summer approached and she needed to earn enough to see her through winter. She might have stayed at home, but the weather was proving to be particularly good. Sat in front of her laptop computer, gazing out of her bedroom window, she decided she ought to get outside and walk.

She had woken with that song in her head. The beat of it at least, the flow, a marching rhythm. She had pulled out her notebook from the clutter of books and sketches on her desk and found Chris' email address. The adolescent scrawl of a Portree teenager who was convinced he was to become the next Scottish rock god but would probably never get a gig beyond the island, and with a few years under his belt, weary from a full-time job and adult responsibilities, would give up on the dream. Chris who also thought Ylva was attracted to him like a fresh slab of lamb flesh.

She didn't want to get in touch, but her curiosity to get more information about the song got the better of her and she emailed him for the lyrics. Hoping she wouldn't come to regret it.

Whilst she'd been digging through her belongings for her notepad, she had also come across the note Helena, her friend at the Broadford tourist office, had given her. She held the sticky note up to the light of the window and considered the name. Leonard MacIntyre. Scottish tourist board. What kind of a man would be called that? And would it be worth contacting him. She couldn't see what use an independent Swedish tour operator would be to a big-wig bureaucrat, but at the same time Maired at Donart Castle had said that she was taking part in this advertising campaign. And if Maired who sold tickets to tourists could take part in a big promotional push, surely it wouldn't be so ridiculous for Ylva to be considered? Perhaps the publicity could be good for her business, and a little extra cash would always be useful. She had sent a polite, vague email off; wondering if she had left it too late.

Dear Leonard MacIntyre,

My name is Ylva Johansson. I run an independent tour service on Skye for customers in English and Swedish. Helena from the Broadford tourist office passed your details on to me and said you wanted to get in touch with people working in the tourist industry on Skye. She mentioned something about advertising. I am not exactly sure how you would like me to help, but please contact me either by email or my mobile if you feel I could help. I look forward to hearing from you soon. Ylva.

Ylva paused as the ground levelled out, and she gazed up to the mountains. She was walking in a large bowl at the foot of the Cullin Mountains, the peak with the drainpipe chasm standing like a child's rocky triangle mountain at the centre front of the distant backdrop. Ahead was the seemingly flat, flowing grassland, cut through by a rocky burn, or river. If driving past from the road part way up on the opposite side of the valley, you wouldn't think there was anything special with the river. Just another mountain stream to pass by on the road on towards Glen Brittle bay and the campsite.

This river was known as the fairy pools river, and was a favourite of Ylva's for walking, photography and painting. The stream crashed its way over a series of rocky waterfalls and cascades; the water an intense mineral blue. It didn't look real on photographs, but when the sun caught the water right, it was as if someone had poured vivid dye in to the mix. The clarity was perfect, and on a sunny day the underwater rock formations and arches could be seen.

She came walking here all year round; an extensive collection of photographs depicting the river's progress under all weather conditions. To come here, switch off all sound and connection with the modern world, and just listen to the run of the water, was bliss.

Ylva had walked a good distance up the side of the river, the opposite direction to the flow of the water, and closer to the mountains, when she decided it was time for lunch. Stepping down from the earth-worn path, she walked onto the bare rock shore of the small river, shrugging off her rucksack. There was a spray of river-smoothed pebbles on the next level, as the water spread out into a relatively shallow, wide pool at the base of a line of small waterfalls. Ylva ate her sandwiches, watched the water and revelled in the fact that she was completely alone.

Untying her laces, she pulled off her hiking boots and socks, discarding them by her rucksack, rolling up the legs of her jeans. Padding barefoot over the rocks, she stepped into the cold water, glad of the sun on her back as the chill bit into her feet. She moved further out into the pool, the blue colour glistening in the sunlight, closer to the waterfalls. The water reached up mid-calf.

She paused, gazing around. Nothing but the sound of moving water. Completely alone. She turned and looked down the river, for a moment feeling as though she was being watched. She had passed one couple walking in the opposite direction on her way here. The little car park had been empty apart from two other vehicles when she had arrived, but perhaps more had turned up now, and were slowly making their way up the side of the river, making slow progress as they were captivated by each photogenic twist of the river.

It felt as though something grabbed at her right ankle. She turned around sharply, the river splashing up into her trousers, waves rocking out across the pool. There was nothing there. She was alone. Her eyes scanned the water. Alone. "Idiot," she muttered to herself, but she didn't feel comfortable enough to stay in the water. Hurriedly she splashed her way back to dry land; the reassuring solid curve of the rock under her feet as she went for her boots.

Further up the twists of the river, on the other side of the water and closer to the mountains, an unclear figure, a man, stood and watched her.

The steady click of knitting needles. The wind blowing gently across the glass. Salt in the air.

Ylva rented a small, whitewashed cottage on a slight rise off a single track dead end road. It was in an area on the edge of Broadford known as Waterloo. Historically this had been a patch of Skye settled by the men coming back home after the battle of Waterloo. It was good to keep the connection to such a major event, for it was quite easy to forget the outer world whilst sat looking at the sea, and even harder to imagine the wider world historically when considering the hard-worked lives of the ancestors of Skye, now just ghosts lingering in the history books and imprinted upon the landscape.

The view from Ylva's living room window rolled down to the sea rocks, the sand and onto the open water of Broadford bay. A view that changed colour with the weather. The bay ran along the length of the town, before the land curled back out into the sea in the distant beyond; a backdrop of mountains pulling up from the earth. Ylva didn't own a television, and her settee was turned to face the window.

Cross legged in the middle, she sat and knitted, gazing out onto the world, her face blank. A drop of knitted material, thirty centimetres in length, hung down from the needles. Ylva wasn't a knitter as such, although she knitted frequently and found the repetitive movement quite soothing. She only did two types of stitches, and she only knitted rectangles and squares – rectangles for scarves and squares to be sewn together for blankets.

There was a knock at the door and Ylva's serene expression wrinkled. She dropped her knitting to the floor and padded bare foot to the front door.

Dougie grinned back as she opened the door. "Ylva!" he burst out, "I was just passing."

"My road's a dead end."

"You know what I mean. Anyway, you don't mind me popping in on you unannounced do you?" The wind picked up and blew through his dark tousled hair. He shrugged deeper into his jacket, hands in pocket to appear that he was suffering more from the chill than he actually was. "You're not busy, are you?"

"No," she said, pushing the door back. "You can come in as long as you don't start speaking Gaelic to me. My head's tired."

Dougie followed her into the cottage, closing the door against the breeze. Ylva's home was something of a contradiction. It had originally been a self-catering cottage for holiday makers, with the usual collection of functional furniture and inexpensive prints of paintings of Scotland adorning the walls. Ylva had done a deal with the woman who owned the cottage, and rented it full time, complete with furnishings. And in some ways it still felt like a holiday home. In other ways, it was completely Ylva, filled with her clutter – stacks of sketch books and ideas for paintings to be completed during the winter months when tourists were few and the weather was not always what might be described as inviting. Seashells, pebbles and rocks lay scattered on windowsills and on the fireplace: gatherings from Ylva's rambles. Wildflowers hung from a ceiling beam, drying out. A basket of balls of wool with grey knitting needles sticking out like fired arrows. Books like flotsam across the room; maps and local guides, handwritten notebooks, jackets and sweaters, homemade woollen scarves. The building was most definitely lived in, settled and cosy, but always with an aftertaste that this was just an extended holiday.

"Come now, don't diss my mother tongue. Gaelic is the language of love."

"Food is the language of love," Ylva muttered.

"That's music."

"Music is the sound." She raised her eyebrows. Dougie could be infuriatingly vague sometimes, but she knew he only did it to wind her up.

Dougie stalked over to the settee, the fine view onto Broadford bay, and picked up Ylva's tangled knitting. "What are you making, here?" he asked, holding it up. "Not another scarf?" he joked.

"I find it meditative."

"And what will you do with this scarf?"

"I don't know." She took the wool off him and settled back onto the settee.

"Can I have it?" Dougie slung his jacket over the back of a wooden chair and slumped down next to her. "I'm sure you've already got one or two yourself."

She smiled to herself. "Sure. Now that I've started I'm thinking I'm not so keen on this colour anyway."

Dougie laughed out loud. "You're too kind. And for that kindness I shall update you on the Broadford gossip."

"I'm sure I already know the local gossip."

"So you know about the cat?"

"The cat?"

"I was over this way visiting a patient in hospital," he began, waving his arm in the general direction of Broadford hospital over the bay. "They were talking about the cat in the hospital."

"Slow day?"

"There's been a dead cat found on Broadford bay." He leant in close, stretching out his arm as if to guide her eye to the exact point, something at this distance would appear not even as a dot.

"What can I say, Dougie," Ylva sighed. "Cats die."

"That they do; but this was murder. It was thrown on a bonfire. Burned alive."

Ylva lowered her knitting. This sounded very familiar. Colm, her friend at the Glen Brittle campsite, had complained about someone roasting a cat on the beach last week. But it wasn't just that. It had been somewhere else.

Dougie didn't notice the expression on her face. "Animal cruelty." He shook his head sadly. "They reckon it's a couple of teenagers. Off their faces on drugs. You know what it's like here."

Ylva pursed her lips together. "Evoking the devil."

He stopped chattering. "Excuse me?"

"Evoking the devil." She dropped her knitting on the floor again and went to the table, flicking through the books and newspapers. "I was reading about it the other night."

"Was this you?"

She rolled her eyes. "Of course not. I'm not interested in the black arts." She found the book. The page was marked with a sticky note, because when she had first read it, she had immediately thought of what Colm had told her, and wondered if it was relevant. "Here it is. The rite of *Taghairm*." She walked back to Dougie, passing him the book as she sat down. "Roasting cats alive to evoke the devil. This one's about a guy and his band of men."

Dougie scanned through the paragraph, flipping the book to check the front cover. Myths and legends, fairy tales and nonsense of the old Scots. Sometimes Ylva's interest in all things Skye could be a little suffocating. "I hope this book isn't giving you ideas."

"Don't worry; I'm not going to do anything. I'm just researching for my tours."

"What, the top ten places in Skye to raise the devil?"

"Well, that's always an idea if times get tough," Ylva said, not seriously. She gazed out of the window. "But it does make you wonder why they're doing it; what they think they're going to achieve. It's not very nice to think that this is being done on my doorstep almost."

"I wouldn't worry about it," Dougie told her, putting the book to one side. "It'll just be a couple of stupid kids who need a kick up the arse. Nothing more to it."

Dear Ylva,

I think you must be a tourist because I don't even know how to say your name. Anyways, the song is called Boys of Bedlam. I'd like to take credit, but it's an old traditional folksong. Still, if you're impressed, why not come to our next gig and we can have a drink afterwards. You know you want to.

I think there's a longer version, but these are the lyrics as I know them.

To see mad Tom of Bedlam, ten thousand miles I'd travel
Mad Maudlin she goes on dirty toes, for to save her shoes from gravel.

(Chorus) Still I sing bonnie boys, bonnie mad boys, Bedlam boys are bonnie
For they all go bare and they live by the air,
And they want no drink nor money.

I went down to Satan's kitchen, for to get me food one morning
There I got souls piping hot, all on the spit a-turning.

(Chorus)

My staff has murdered giants, and my bag a long knife carries
For to cut mince pies from children's thighs, with which to feed the fairies.

(Chorus)

Spirits white as lightning, shall on my travels guide me
The moon would quake and the stars would shake,
where ever they espied me.

(Chorus)

No gypsy slut nor doxy, shall win my mad Tom from me
I'll weep all night, the stars I'll fight, the fray will well
become me.

(Chorus)

And when that I have murdered, the Man-In-The-Moon
to a powder
His staff I'll break, his dog I'll bake, there'll howl no
demon louder.

(Chorus)

So drink to Tom of Bedlam, he'll fill the seas in barrels
I'll drink it all, all brewed with gall, with Mad Maudlin I will
travel.

(Chorus – repeat fade out)

Seeing you, Chris

The morning had started very early with frenzied phone calls. Bizarrely early, and Ylva couldn't quite understand the need for urgency. But, she supposed, as she stuffed her hands into her jacket pockets and stood up against the wind sweeping over the Trotternish, they probably had a schedule to keep, and fitting it in with her own was obviously not that easy with the approaching summer months.

The Trotternish, the north-easterly peninsula of Skye, was something of a geologist's dream, and a day's touring potential of dinosaur find sites, dinosaur footprints, dramatic scenery, old men and hidden cornices of fairies. Ylva was currently in the Quiraing – a violently rocky and jagged upland landscape of drama that looked fitting for the backdrop for some glossy, high-production fantasy film. The wind was blowing quite fiercely, and even though she was relatively warm, she felt the need for a woollen hat, to try and keep her hair down under some control.

The area had more than its fair share of local legend and folklore, as Ylva had been reading last night just before Leonard MacIntyre of the Scottish tourist board had called her. She had been a little surprised to read about another old incident of *Taghairm* – roasting cats alive to invoke the devil – had been performed on the Trotternish. Albeit further down the road, near Storr, but it was said that the robber chief still roamed the Trotternish, having been rejected from hell for a good deed once performed, and refusing to go to heaven out of a desire to join his robber band in hell. There was something about the scenery up here that almost made you believe such stories could be true.

Callum MacIntosh, a curly-haired Scottish photographer in his early forties, was next after Ylva in the single-file hiking line. A rucksack of camera gear strapped to his back, a tripod carried casually over his shoulder as if it were no weight at all, he watched the strands of Ylva's hair whip out from her hat and collar, and the seeds of an idea began to form.

Behind Callum was his assistant, then Leonard MacIntyre the tourist board personified, and finally a silent woman, for whom Ylva could discern no obvious reason as to why she was here.

Callum paused, the line backing up after him. "Hamish, pass me the camera. I'll get a few sound bites from Yuellva now. Yuellva!" he shouted after her. "Slow down a wee bit."

She stopped, twisted to look back at the crumpled end of the train. They were walking on a relatively narrow path, quite level, across a steep bank – the first part of the route from the car park at the top of the Quiraing. Strands of hair whipped across her face.

"Give us a sound bite of the Quiraing; imagine we're your tour group. As you're walking. I'll keep a few meters back to get some of the scenery in."

"And would you like this factual or poetic?" she joked. Leonard had explained on the first phone conversation yesterday evening that he wanted to get two series of images from the people chosen to represent the Skye tourist industry. One would be factual – closer to what the person did, real experiences of Skye people could hope to gain on their holiday; the other more poetic and artistic; focused in on the image rather than information. He had a vision for this campaign, he told her. There would be film footage and photographic stills – they would be hitting television, newspapers, magazines, the Internet and possibly large posters for tourist offices. Ylva inwardly cringed at the thought of her picture appearing in an advertisement for 'come to Scotland'.

Callum grinned. "This is the factual bit. I think I know what I want for the other shots."

Leonard looked a little put out at this comment. Ylva's participation hadn't been particularly well planned. After discussion and comparison of schedules last night, they had realised the only full day for working with Ylva would be the next day, which barely left enough time to get the crew mobilised, let alone plan out the storyboards for the shoots. Callum had been unperturbed by the short notice, and having quickly rung Ylva himself, had reassured Leonard that he'd work it all out on the day, whatever the weather. He was used to working in the moment. Which was fine, but Leonard was supposed to be in charge of this project and he wished Callum would let him in on his moments of artistic lucidity.

"Ok, we're filming you."

She suddenly felt shy, and turned her back on the audience. How was she supposed to behave now? What did they want her to say? "What do you want me to do?"

"Start walking for one," Callum answered. "Just act natural; as you would with a tour. Tell us about where we are."

This felt very forced. She started to walk again and her hiking boot slid down a protruding rock, making her wobble momentarily. "*Gud*," She swore under her breath. "Don't show that bit," she added. "People will think I'm drunk on the job."

"Don't worry; we'll save it for the section on the whisky."

"Thanks."

"So, come on, where are we?"

"This is the Quiraing." She reached out with her arms as if going to hug the vista ahead all at once. "We're taking a short walk across the ridge here to go and see some of the rocky formations. We've got a needle, a prison and a table."

The filming continued thus, with breaks to walk over the more demanding sections. They went up onto the table, which was a little harder with the steep, eroded route. The soundless woman – whoever she was – said that she wasn't walking up there and would head back to their vehicle to wait for them. No one seemed to be bothered about her departure.

The table was a large, flat area of grass surrounded by monstrous shafts of rocks and formations as if it were an unturned bug and they were walking territorially across the belly. It was told that locals used to hide cattle up here, and play shinty (careful you don't run off the edge) but these days it was a beauty spot.

Ylva had her photograph taken in countless variations up on the table, in every case as an aside to the stunning scenery. The wind played to their favour, pushing the clouds on swiftly. There was good visibility, and the constant movement of cloud cover played a mottled patchwork of light and dark across the undulating green and rock-strewn stretches down from them towards the shores in the distance. Callum had been particularly enthused by the hour they spent up on the table, promising to email Ylva copies of the pictures, and chattering of how much he hadn't realised he missed the wild open landscape of Scotland. A defector-Scot, Leonard had called him, referencing to the fact that Callum now lived in the north of England.

Finishing with work on the Trotternish, Callum announced to the group that he wanted to complete this day-long session on Broadford Bay. Everyone but Hamish the assistant looked mortified at the suggestion as Callum merrily put his gear back into the sleek expensive four-wheel-drive jeep Leonard had rolled up in outside Ylva's cottage that morning. They had driven to the north of the island all the way from Broadford. Granted, they would have to go back the same way eventually to leave Skye, but they still had two other people to photograph on the island and would be staying for the next few days. To drive back all that distance, well over an hour and a half, seemed arse-first. They should have done Broadford Bay first. The woman, still nameless, was ready to get to her hotel room in Portree and was thoroughly irritated by the suggestion. Ylva, who was a resident of Broadford, really didn't want to have her neighbours watching her give a tour of Broadford to a cameraman.

To her relief, as Callum explained on the drive back down through the island, he didn't want her to give a tour of Broadford. In fact, as this was to be the artistic segment, talking didn't seem necessary; this was to be a visual experience. Which probably would have been easier, when

Ylva understood this was going to be as a proper modelling job now.

They parked up at the southern end of the bay, a little way down the dead-end road where Ylva lived. The woman, who it now appeared was a self-styled wardrobe mistress and supposed makeup genius, pulled a full-length, sleeveless ball gown out of a box in the back as if this was the kind of thing one would find in any well kitted out jeep. She gave Ylva a sour, assessing look, before commenting about the differences in waist sizes and throwing the dress at Ylva.

"What do you want me to do with this?" Ylva looked horrified. Helping the Scottish tourist board was not supposed to including frolicking in front of her neighbours in a ball dress on the beach. No amount of money was going to be worth this.

"Get in it."

"What, out here in the open?"

"I thought you were Swedish," the woman said, making it sound like a challenge, "I thought that kind of thing didn't bother you people."

"And you've obviously been getting your information from too many porn films."

Her eyes narrowed ever so slightly. "Be nice. Or I may accidentally stab you with a safety pin when I'm sorting that waist out."

Ylva threw her jacket into the open passenger door of the jeep. "*Jävla häxa*," she grumbled. Bloody witch. She didn't know what she'd done to engage the woman's fury.

Shedding her hiking boots and jumper, she was down to socks, jeans and a vest top. Drawing the back zip all the way down, she shrugged her way into the dress, the jeans making the gauze, aquamarine layers bunch up around her hips. Holding the front of the dress up against her as if the sight of her bra would cause a public flogging, she pulled her vest top off and slipped her arms through the straps. As she unzipped her jeans and started to wiggle them down to her ankles, the woman roughly pulled the zip up her back.

"It is too flabby."

"Excuse me?" Ylva twisted sharply, almost loosing balance as her legs were still knotted up in her trousers.

She was ignored as the woman took the waist of the dress and folded fabric tight back, fixing with a safety pin. Smooth against her skin, the bodice was starting to look as though it had been poured onto her.

Ylva was passed a long piece of semi-transparent blue-green material, an extended shawl as light as light itself. As she unfolded it, the wind picked up the edge and it was whipped out like a flag, a horizontal flame.

"I'm going to pin this to one side of the dress," the woman told her, fixing one corner of the shawl to the dress bodice top. "You'll only loose it otherwise."

"I'm not that careless." The shawl stretched out to its full length then was blown back ungraciously onto Ylva's head.

"You'd better get onto the beach," she was told. "We don't want this to take all day."

Barefooted once on the sand, Ylva joined Callum where he'd set up camp, sticking her socks in his camera bag. The wind blew in off the sea, whipping through her hair, her skirts and that stupid shawl that was good for nothing. With Leonard and Hamish stationed at intervals further along the beach to keep dog walkers and tourists off the sand for as long as possible, Callum was on his own; a camera slung over one shoulder; a steadycam video camera in his hands.

"Right, Yuellva," Callum looked up. "I'm thinking ethereal and dreamlike; I'm thinking magical misty Skye." He burst out laughing when he saw Ylva's expression. "Leonard's words; not mine," he told her. "I think he's looking for something atmospheric."

"And me being battered by the wind will achieve that?"

"Don't worry; I'll make you look good. Now, I'll be angling this so we have the sea and the far side of the bay in shot. I want to try and keep as much of Broadford out of this as possible. Certainly the supermarket and car park over there. We'll walk so far out across the sand, I'll get close ups with the film and the camera. Then I want you to wait till I get back across there," he waved his arm at the burnt-looking seaweed-covered rocks that edged the sand of the bay. "I've got a good zoom on this one."

"And what do you want me to do?"

"Walk ahead of me. And not that frogmarch you were doing off up the mountains. A casual stroll pace. If I have to run after you to keep up, a soundtrack of heavy breathing to this isn't going to give it the right sort of connotations."

"Surely you can dub that sort of thing out."

He smiled lightly. "You're not comfortable doing this are you?"

"Not really. I'm wondering why I agreed to it in the first place."

"Because you only live once," he egged her on. "A few years ago I would never have thought I would have been working on projects like these either. Now, keep ahead of me, and every few metres, turn around. I don't mean stand on the spot and twirl; turn around as you keep on walking. Not too fast. Let the wind take this shawl. We're looking to create a kind of ripple, water effect. Oh, and, Yuellva?"

"What?"

"Try not to scrumple your face up like that against the wind. Think serene."

Ylva walked on ahead, trying to look serene and mysterious. The wind caught the shawl and blew it away from her body like a kite. She flicked her hair off her face and looked out to sea. She wondered how Callum had come to work on a project like this. Leonard had mentioned that he was very experienced, competent. He'd been all over the world making documentaries; filming and photographing history as it blew up – riots and protests, events, takeovers. The world history captured in a second. And now this.

She was conscious of being watched. Beside Callum, a few meters back, she could feel the eyes on her, from behind. As she turned, she glanced at land, and the car park where a small gathering of people had collected, stood watching from the edge. Held back by Hamish who looked as though he was enjoying the authority. This attention pricked her, made her paranoid. It even felt as though the sea itself was watching.

Callum left her and headed back to the edge of the bay so he could get some more panoramic shots of the coastline. When in position, he signalled to Ylva to start walking again. She turned and made tracks in the sand, a diagonal route away and across to the tide line where the sea lapped at the shells and strands of ripped seaweed it had brought up. She was walking alone on an empty beach, but she still felt as though she was being observed from a close distance.

She paused, glancing over her shoulder, she looked back to the corner of the bay where Callum was. The wind tore the shawl out of her grasp, a sudden burst of energy. She stretched out her arm, twisting an edge between fingers before turning right around to continue walking. She supposed she would just keep on walking until she was told to stop. She had no idea how this was all going to turn out.

They were late. They were constantly late to these get-togethers. Morag always blamed the bus, but Ylva was sure it was just that she was disorganised and missed the bus she should have caught, forced into taking the later one. And so Ylva loitered in the middle of Broadford waiting for the bus from Portree to arrive so that she and Morag could drive off in her VW camper van.

"Do you mind if I smoke?" Morag asked as she grubbed around in her handbag.

"Yes!" Ylva stressed. They had this conversation every time she gave Morag a lift anywhere. "This is where I bring my visitors."

"They're not here now."

"No, but I am."

"Ach, well," Morag sighed, snapping the bag shut. "I'll just have to wait till we get there."

"You want to crash at mine tonight?"

"It'll probably be the morrow when we head back, but yes, that would be grand. I took the bairns over to my mother's."

The bairns. It never ceased to boggle Ylva. She was a year older than Morag and yet Morag already had two young children. She had been married as well, technically still was, but the couple had split up just after the birth of the second child and Morag had been on her own since.

Pulling down the sun guard, despite the swiftly vanishing daylight, Morag checked her make up in the mirror. "Want to make sure I'm looking my best. I might be able to get myself a nice young man at this party."

Ylva laughed out loud.

"That's what my mother told me before I left," she said with a grin.

"Well, we both know who's going to be at this party; so we both know that there won't be any of that kind of thing going on." Ylva said. They were driving through the dusk to a beach party on Glen Brittle bay – one of Colm's around-the-bonfire gatherings for members of the mountain rescue team, plus spouses, girlfriends and boyfriends and the odd other associate – namely Ylva and Morag. Neither of whom was in the mountain rescue team or in a relationship with such a person, but because Ylva knew Colm so well, and Morag knew Ylva, they qualified for an invite. "There'll be no eligible young bachelors there."

"There's a few single men."

"Doesn't mean you'd want to chase them."

"Well, Colm…"

Ylva's eyes widened at the half-mentioned comment. She drove over a cattle grid as they passed by a small farm, the vibrations rattling through the silence. She glanced over at Morag. "Colm's so old; he'll soon be fifty. You're not seriously thinking of chasing him?"

"Oh no; not anymore."

"Not anymore? As in you were?"

"Well, there was last summer, but, you know…" Morag drifted off and became particularly interested in the clasp of her handbag. She regretted she'd brought this up.

The revelation was news to Ylva. "What are you talking about last summer for?"

Morag shrugged and pondered for a moment whether there was a way of wriggling out of this one. Probably not now that she had made such a leading comment. And it was only Ylva – she wouldn't cause trouble with information like this. "We had a bit of a fling last summer. Very short lived."

"You're joking?" She coughed on the words, as if they had to be untrue. It hardly seemed credible. Ylva had no idea anything had gone on between them. Colm had said nothing. He had never even hinted that he was seeing a woman of any description to her; and because of their history dating back to Sweden, she saw herself – perhaps deluded – as a confidant. "I had no idea."

"Aye, well, we didn't broadcast it." Morag sighed. "You know what people are like for gossiping. And there's no point putting yourself through all that, what with the wee ones and the age thing, if it's no' going anywhere."

Ylva stared straight out of the windscreen, concentrating on the road ahead. "I suppose not," she agreed, not really knowing. Not that any of this was her business, but it was like being pushed out into the cold, to discover something like this about two of your friends. As if finding out that they only marked you down as a casual acquaintance; whilst you were merely skipping along thinking you were in one another's confidences. It just went to show how you didn't really know anyone.

"You won't tell anyone I mentioned it?"

"Oh, come on," Ylva rolled her eyes, forcing herself to stop being so self-involved. It wasn't a snub to her that this secret affair had been none of her business. "I do have a bit of class, you know."

When Ylva pulled the van up at the end of a line of cars, she could see they definitely were the last to arrive. The bonfire was blazing, the images of people illuminated in orange outline against the inky dusk. Colm and a couple of the men were working two small barbecues off to the side. Smoke twisted and blew up into the night sky.

Morag got out of the passenger seat, taking up her plastic bag of cans of lagers from the foot well. Putting a cigarette in the corner of her mouth, she lit up. "Oh, I was dying for that." She watched as Ylva wandered around to the back of the van. "Are you not going to get a wee bit cold there?"

Ylva, who was dressed in shorts and a long sleeved, flowing top with an angular line, shook her head as she picked up her belongings. "I have my Russian soldier coat, I'll be fine."

"Your Russian what?"

"Oh, it's just what Dougie calls it." She explained, taking out the navy blue coat, complete with brass buttons and rectangular epaulettes; a high collar and a length that reached the top of her ankles. "When I get cold I'll disappear into this."

"And what exciting treats have you got in your flasks?"

She hooked the woven bag over the crook of her elbow. "Tea and orange juice – in separate flasks, of course." She grinned and waved her keys. "Designated driver."

"I know," Morag rolled her eyes. "We'll have to get ourselves to a caelidh in Portree. You can sleep over at mine and you won't have to worry about all that."

"I'm going to have to get something to eat; I'm starving," Morag told Ylva as she hurried off in the direction of the barbecues. Ylva wandered at her own pace, drawn to the warmth of the bonfire. A few of the mountain rescuers were stood in a loose group gossiping. As Ylva drew closer she overheard Ronny, a middle-aged, bearded Scot with ruddy cheeks say something about killing cats. He paused in his rather seriously toned gossip as he saw her.

"Evening, Illvar. On time as usual."

"It was Morag's fault."

"You always say that. I was just telling Alan here about the recent spate of animal cruelty we've been having down our way. You heard about those cats being roasted alive?"

"Oh yes, on Broadford Bay."

"Oh, aye, there's those ones as well."

"As well? So you're talking about the one Colm found?"

Ronny's eyebrows drew close, threatening to become entangled. "I didn't know Colm had found one. I'm taking about the fire they found up by the old marble mines."

"I didn't know about that. The only ones I've heard about were on beaches."

"Good job no one's brought a cat to this," Alan joked, pointing his bottle at the bonfire.

"Strange going on." Ronny rubbed his beard.

"Strange goings on at the beach?" Dougie, who was a part time member of the mountain rescue, appeared at the edge of the gathering. "You're telling me. I had to visit a patient at the hospital. I was in Broadford in the afternoon and there was a fella there telling us we weren't to go on the beach. Some crazy had gotten lost on the way to the opera."

Ylva eyelids sank, heavy with embarrassment. She hadn't quite gotten over the beach episode, only a couple of hours old, and didn't need Dougie making light hearted fun of her. It was typical that he would have seen it.

Despite living in Broadford, Ronny had obviously missed the spectacle. "Who's that then?"

"Ylva here."

Ronny looked over at her. "You were at an opera on the beach?"

"No," she groaned. "I was just in a frock on the bay. I've gotten involved in this tourist promotion thing. They have footage of me running around waving my arms and getting excited on the Quiraing table."

"In an opera dress?"

"No, I was suitably attired for that one. They said they're going to bring it all to Portree in a few weeks when it's ready. Have a proper opening for it all."

"And this is for the Scottish tourist board? I suppose it'll be good promotion for that wee business of yours."

"I hope so."

The gathering got going – food, drink and chatter. Night closed in around them, the heat from the fire proof against the chill. Stars overhead glittered. Colm had his guitar out, someone else had brought a fiddle and the music soon started up. It was quite warm near the fire, and Ylva sat on her coat for the time, happy with her cups of tea and hot dogs. She watched as Morag said something to Colm between songs, probably just a request, and she honestly couldn't see anything between them. It was hard to credit the story.

Getting up from the sand, she kicked off her sandals and stretched her legs. She wandered away from the group and towards the sea. The tide wouldn't reach the bonfire, but the walk was shorter than it had been when she had gone for a paddle earlier. Dipping her feet into the dying waves, she hissed as the cold cut into her, draining the warmth stored up from the bonfire. The water lapped up around her skin as she wandered out into the sea, stopping as it reached mid calf. She stood still, feeling the sea breeze brush her hair back off her shoulders, listening to the sound of the great body of water out in the darkness, moonlit waves breaking through the background.

Turning, she looked back to the gathering – mostly locals born and bred with a few who had moved to the island in the last couple of years interspersed. The colour of the fire glowed like life against the black.

"I've been looking for you."

Ylva let out a small cry as an unfamiliar voice broke into her quiet contemplation. Stumbling in her place, away from the fire, water splashing nosily up her legs. She looked back out to sea. A few meters away a man she didn't know stood in the water. He was a little further out than Ylva, the waves brushing by mid thigh. His misshapen clothes hung on his body, his dark hair a tangled mess. He grinned at her, two teeth missing.

"Ylva?"

Dougie's voice from the beach. Distracted, she looked over her shoulder. He was stood at the edge of the water, shoes just out of reach of the tide, hands in jacket pockets. Slightly sheepish. She turned back to the stranger, but he had gone. Confused, she turned around on the spot but she couldn't see where he had gone.

"Are you all right?"

"Yes, but that man." She backed out of the water to the sand. Grains of sand immediately sticking to her wet skin.

"What man?"

"The one stood in the water with me."

Dougie squinted through the moonlight. Was this some kind of game she was playing with him? "There's no one else here."

"But I saw him."

"Moonlight playing tricks on your eyes."

"I was sure…"

"Ylva, are you mad at me?"

"What?" she turned, for the first time giving him her full attention. He didn't appear to have any interest, even feigned, at what she thought she had seen in the water. "Mad at you? I don't know what you're talking about."

"Well, me mentioning your thing on the beach. I hope you didn't think I was being malicious."

"Jesus, Dougie, have you been drinking?" she walked over to him. "That's never stopped you making fun before. Anyway, this is going to be a major advertising campaign. They're having an exhibition in the Portree tourist office as well. Everyone's going to see this sooner or later."

"I'm sure it will look great."

"Well, that remains to be seen." She shivered as the wind blew up the back of her legs. It wasn't quite the weather for shorts. "I need my coat; let's head back."

"You've brought the coat you pinched off that extra?"

"That extra?" she asked, linking arms with him as they headed back to the bonfire.

"You know, Russian guard number two; used to get regular work on James Bond films."

"Oh, that one, of course," she nodded. "I get confused. I take so many things from hard-up actors you know."

"Someone's got to keep them in their place, though, haven't they? Got to keep them on their toes."

Ulla Britt Todd had been feeling her age ever since the death of her husband. When the legalities and necessities were complete, she sold their home in Canada, the furniture and her ties, and moved back to her hometown, Uppsala in Sweden. She had thought a return to her roots would be reenergising; bring Ulla Britt back to life, perhaps back to a carefree younger time, that amazing feeling of youth when everything looked so promising. She'd been looking for her *smultronstället*, but instead she stumbled on the cobbles and realised she'd been left behind.

The Sweden of today was not the Sweden she'd emigrated from forty years ago. It had moved on, and she felt a stranger in her home. This was her birth place, yet it rushed by as if they were mere passing acquaintances. The students flew by on bicycles, not old enough to be away from their mothers. Ulla Britt was most definitely seventy five years old.

Still, even ruins with no obvious purpose could be beautiful, she mused as she stood on the grass before Armadale Castle. There was always something interesting to be found. In a technical sense, this castle served little purpose: roofless and slowly crumbling, it wasn't going to keep anyone's head dry, and it was hardly ready to prove protection against an attack. Yet there was something calming about the site, and it would be a good place for sketching if only she hadn't left her drawing pads in the mini bus.

On the grass sat her youngest granddaughter, Elena, at seventeen – still with her chubby-cheeked adolescent face and long straight blonde hair. She had not been happy on the ferry crossing from Mallaig, and despite the short travel time, she was still complaining that she had not adjusted to dry land. She was certainly trying her best now, sprawled out across the grass with a trashy teenage horror book in her hands.

Elena was the only true remnant of Canada on this trip, daughter to Ulla Britt's son, a family based in Ontario. Taken away from her parents for a summer trip to Scotland, for Ulla Britt had decided she wanted to travel with all of her grandchildren together. A journey of something different. It would give the grandchildren a chance to get to know each other, and for Elena to practice her Swedish with natives. Her cousins, Karl and Harriet, were the offspring of a wild child, who had moved back to the land of her ancestors as soon she was allowed, falling pregnant at fifteen and refusing to continue a relationship with the father, let alone get married. Karl had turned thirty this year, and Ulla Britt had been doubtful he would readily accompany them on this trip to Scotland. He had surprised her by being the most eager of all the grandchildren. Harriet had been the longest to be brought to the suggestion, but Karl had told his grandmother on the ferry out across the Sound of Sleat that there was a boy in Karlstad who was distracting Harriet from anything that did not involve his immediate circle. Their mother was worried that Harriet was too young for such intense plans – which made Ulla Britt laugh, because Susana had given birth to Karl just before her sixteenth birthday; and Harriet was already twenty five.

And there, loitering respectfully in the background but always ready to hand, their guide for the week so they would have no need to plan or think; a lucky find, a Swedish tour guide – and a native at that – so that they could travel abroad but still speak Swedish and let Elena practice. Ylva Johansson, the Swedish Skye guide, stood near the restored section on the castle grounds where a small art gallery was housed. Ulla Britt watched from a distance, envying youth and opportunity. Ylva was tying back her hair, idly watching Elena read. The older woman scanned across, to see Harriet talking at her brother, and Karl watching Ylva. He'd been quite taken with her, even before they had disembarked from the ferry and realised that the blonde woman in jeans and an oddly shaped lime-green top was to be their guide for the week.

Letting her arms drop, Ylva closed her eyes and savoured the sun on the back of her neck. After the chilly beach party, it was sweet to feel the warmth of the sun again. She'd checked the forecast before driving down to the south of the island to pick up her group of Swedes for the coming week. Aside from a couple of short lived showers, it looked promising – a particularly stable blip of good weather for an island renowned for its changeability, but more than that, at least twenty different types of fog and mist.

She slowly crossed the grass towards the old woman, the head of the party and the lady who had arranged this week with her in communication by email. Ylva was surprised when the woman had told her that she was seventy five – she didn't look it, and she was certainly prepared for walking and outdoor activities.

"*Are you feeling tired from the journey up here?*" Ylva asked in Swedish.

Ulla Britt smiled weakly and shrugged her shoulders. "*A little, but we did not come all the way to Scotland to just rest. I want to spend time with my family. I want to explore this place. I'd like to do some painting as well. You did say you'd take us to some good places for painting.*"

"*Of course, but not on the day you arrive. This is the very far south of the island and it will be a long drive up to Portree. I thought it was just as well that we look around this area a little before we head up to the bed and breakfast.*"

"*Well, it's certainly a fine building,*" the old woman commented, looking up at the castle. "*I imagine it was a stunning building in its time. But is there much to see inside it? I see that part is built up.*"

"*Not as much as the next castle we'll visit. There's a small heritage centre here. They've got an exhibition on at the moment.*"

"*An exhibition.*"

"*Paintings.*"

"*Oh really?*" Ulla Britt perked up a little. "*And I think you mentioned somewhere on your website that you paint.*"

Ylva held up her hands, laughing. *"Not my exhibition. This one is quite good. Do you want to go and take a look?"*

"Yes, I will see if I can find some ideas for this week."

They walked across the grass towards the visitor centre, making polite, inoffensive conversation. As they reached the door, Ylva felt how out of place their Swedish was; one of the castle guides glancing across at them. She came over to welcome them, and as genuine as the woman was, it irritated Ylva, because she spoke to them standing on presumptions, making her words that little bit clearer and over pronounced. It reminded Ylva that she wasn't of this island. It was stupid and petty, but it always got her defences up, and she would reply in her strongest Scottish accent, as trained by her mother. It was times like this that she wished her Gaelic had come along enough so that she could turn around and speak back to these people in the old language of the island. It would catch some people out, because not everyone living on Skye spoke fluent Gaelic. But her dedication to her studies grew and waned in irregular fluctuations, and she had not yet progressed from fumbling awkwardness.

The woman's question; hello and welcome – is it your first time on the island? – was still irking Ylva early the next morning as she was walking along the front of Portree harbour. That look as if they'd just come off the banana boat. Sticking out was something she usually relished, but lately this feeling of being on the outside, not quite part of something, was getting increasingly infuriating.

As she started up the steps to the road – Portree the town rolled down quite a steep slope to the seafront – she bumped into Callum MacIntosh, the photographer working on the Scottish tourist board promotions. "Yuellva!" he greeted her, looking more excited to be meeting her than she would have expected after a single day of working together. Perhaps if he had fallen madly in love with her, and had feared they might never meet again, he could have behaved like this; but that kind of emotion lived in melodramatic novels and Ylva was sure she'd heard some reference to a wife back home during the day. And if it was neither love nor the joyful shock of a reunion, then something was up.

"Callum," she nodded to him. "Nice to see you again. How is the photography tour of Skye coming on?"

"Not bad. We've just got one more fella to do, then we've finished with our Skye people. It's looking very good," he assured her. "Although your pictures were the damnedest thing. I was wanting to see you about it. I'm going to have to airbrush some of them quite a lot."

Ylva felt her smile drop, dead weights pulling the corners of her mouth down. Everyone knew airbrushing was common in fashion photography – all those models and actresses were only human and suffered from uneven skin tone and blocked pores with the best of the human race, but Callum made it sound as though the sight was so terrible they would need to clip out another girl's face and paste it onto Ylva's body.

"I don't mean that," he said drolly, guessing what she was thinking. "You're a very photogenic woman, and I'm sure your man tells you that on a regular basis. And if he doesn't he should. What I'm talking about is something else. Look, I've got some prints to show you – I told you I was hoping to see you..."

He chattered on and Ylva didn't have the heart to interrupt and correct the facts. There wasn't a man. No one told her she was photogenic; or anything else for that matter.

"I could have sworn we got that beach at a good moment and kept all the people off whilst we were shooting."

"There's someone in the background?"

Callum nodded as he unfolded a couple of sheets of computer paper; colour images printed off.

"Well surely it'll be a speck in the distance?"

"If only," Callum said. "But even so, we were looking for an atmosphere of dramatic wilderness. But honest to God, I can't believe we missed her." He passed the pictures to Ylva. "She's standing right there in the sea; close enough to see her face. She'll have to be digitally removed."

The picture, only a computer print out, but even so, was very professional. As if it had been plucked from an advertising campaign already running. Ylva was impressed, although a little disconcerted to see her own face stare back at her. Perhaps ten metres or so beyond, in the shallows of the sea, another woman was standing. The bottom of her long dress was lost in the water, a dark stain soaking upwards. Her chestnut brown curls blew in the wind, and she looked quite seriously in Ylva's direction. There was something familiar about her.

"I can't believe I didn't notice her stood there."

"And she's in all the pictures? What about your film? Won't that be harder to delete her out?"

Callum shook his head. "She must have realised she was in the way and got out of shot quick, because she's only in a few of the photographs, and not on the film at all. I still can't believe I never saw her there. I like to think I've got a bit of an eye for detail."

Ylva tapped the paper thoughtfully. "I think I've seen her before."

"She's a mate of yours?"

"Oh no, nothing like that. I think she's a tourist. I saw her hitchhiking just outside of Uig the other day." Standing in the rain, thumbing for a lift and then disappearing when Ylva pulled over onto the side of the road. "But you're right; it is odd that we never noticed her paddling in the sea. They're very good photographs though," she passed the papers back.

"Ach no, you hang on to them." Callum told her, shouldering his bag again. "I've got to get on, and you can keep them as a memento. Although I'm sure Leonard'll have something a bit more glossy for you all when this campaign's finalised."

Ylva pretended to grimace. "I'll look forward to that."

Claigan Coral Beaches are a long way up Skye, on the tip of the middle prong of the north-westerly arm. Green, gently undulating land rolls neatly to the coast and into the sea, which is a gleaming turquoise when the sun is in the mood to shine in the right direction. The beaches are a brilliant white, and from a distance you'd be forgiven for thinking that you'd hit the Caribbean; or more realistically one of the machair of Scotland (of which there are actually none on Skye). The colour and consistency isn't actually sand, and neither is it really a coral beach in the strictest sense you might expect. The beach is made up of something called maerl, which is the calcified remains of a kind of sea algae. Knobbly, strangely shaped pieces of calcified forms, bizarre chalk perhaps, that give a crunch underfoot.

And whilst the name, Claigan Coral Beaches, may give the wrong impression of what lies in the water; just as a distant view is misleading as to what kind of beach it is; the site had been of geological interest for decades and was well marked on the guide books and trails; standing out as something a little different.

Ylva stood at the top of the beach and savoured the sea breeze against her face. They had come up over the hillock, past the rocky promontories, and down onto the beach. On the way over they'd passed a couple sitting in the grass behind the crumbling stone wall; the girl lying on her side and being patted by her partner. She didn't look particularly happy; he didn't seem to know what to do. He'd smiled politely as Ylva had given them a curious stare walking by – a bad dinner last night; the effects of food poisoning today. Every tour operator's nightmare, Ylva supposed as she led her small party of Swedes down to the shoreline.

Ulla Britt was walking against the edge of the dying waves against the shore, arm in arm with her youngest granddaughter, Elena. Harriet had headed off to a hillock further up, showing a sudden passion for photography and declaring that she had found her first inspiration for some great shots so far this holiday. Day two and things were looking better.

Karl, the eldest of the grandchildren and even Ylva's senior by a couple of years, stuffed his hands into his jacket pockets and slunk across to their guide for the week. His shaggy, dark brown hair flapping in the breeze; a complexion that screamed of clean and a face that looked as though it had been designed in neat Nordic perfection with not even a single hair out of place.

"It's quite some place here," he started, not entirely sure how to broach a conversation with her that she would understand to be genuine and friendly rather than politely professional. Something said to fit the situation, cover an awkward silence, but nothing she would be interested in. He looked out across the beach. *"It reminds me a bit of Fårö."*

Ylva nodded slowly. *"I can see where you're coming from, but it's not as much of a lunar landscape as Fårö,"* she said, thinking of the small island to the north of the Swedish island Gotland, out in the Baltic Sea. *"That just feels endless."*

Karl watched her, feeling the fascination built. Carefully considered every word, her accent. The way she carried herself as she stood and looked out to the sea. *"You're from further north, aren't you?"*

"Sorry?"

"In Sweden. You're a northerner."

"Well, Umeå. You can get further north than that."

"I'd call that proper north."

"All right," she laughed. *"I'm a northern Swede, then."*

"Now living in Scotland. You know, I'm impressed by what's set up here. I mean, this island, there's not actually that much here."

"Excuse me," Ylva scoffed. *"There's a lot here. I've lived on Skye two years and I've still not finished exploring."*

"But there's not that many physical things; you know, castles and museums, culture and all that. A lot of it is the

natural world – geology and mountains, scenery and walking."

"And god bless it," Ylva finished.

"But this is the thing. We've got the same in Sweden. But everyone wants to come here, and no one wants to go to Sweden."

"You've obviously not travelled as much as you should have," Ylva pointed out. *"Sweden as a nation just does not get tourism. And definitely not as a promotional activity. Outside of Scandinavian, discounting the people of Holland who seem to be a case in their own right; who thinks to go on holiday to Sweden? No one. Swedes seem to take it for granted that the whole world knows everything about them and so there's no reason for us to self-promote. Yet a lot of the world thinks we're an ice-locked forest inhabited by ABBA clones."* She shrugged to herself. *"We could have a booming tourist industry, but we're too non-confrontational. And maybe that's good in a way. You can miss the peace and quiet.. Tourists can be incredibly trying after a while."*

Karl watched as she broke into a grin. *"I hope we're not trying yet."*

"Not yet."

"Even so, I am impressed. What you've got here. You run this business on your own, right?"

"I do," she nodded. *"And what do you do?"*

"Me? Oh, I'm just working at the university library in Linköping at the moment. It's crap trying to get a job related to your degree. I suppose I should move to Stockholm to stand a chance," he sighed, *"But I really don't want to live in such a big place."*

"And what was your degree in?"

"Economics." He smiled lop sidedly. *"I would have loved to do geology – that's my passion. But I thought economics would help me in the job market. Be the sensible choice. But I've not had a lot of success since I graduated. I think I should have done what was interesting – at least I'd have some good memories of my student days."*

"Something will work out," she said – the standard response in the face of someone disillusioned with life; but both parties knew that there was no guarantee of anything promising ever coming up. *"But if you're interested in geology, then there should be plenty to see this week,"* she continued, steering them in a more mutually agreeable direction.

"Yes, I was reading up about it online. The diatomite and marble industries on Skye..."

"Marble, yes." Ylva smiled to herself. *"One of the few Gaelic words I've managed to learn easily. Marmor."* Marble. She glanced over at Karl. *"You know it's the same in Swedish and Gaelic?"*

He smiled back. *"You know what; I didn't know that."*

Whilst on the north-west coast of Skye, the natural progression for a day's touring was Donart Castle and village, followed up by a visit to Neist Point lighthouse. She hadn't been out that way since she had chaperoned the two pensioners, Agnes and Mildred, from Northumberland.

After the coral beaches, Ylva had driven the group back a short distance. They had taken a short walk around Donart village and the surrounding countryside, taking in a couple of old churches and a memorial stone. Lunch at the café in the Donart Castle car park, before going into the castle gardens. They had an hour for the castle and gardens before Ylva had arranged for a boat trip from the jetty at the foot of the castle out to see the seals. Ylva didn't like to chaperone people too much, particularly a family that appeared to be ready to get used to spending time together again. There was urgency in Ulla Britt in particular that this was going to work. They agreed where to meet for the boat ride, and at what time, and Ylva left them to amble through to the castle at their own pace.

As often seemed to happen when she roamed the castle grounds, waiting in limbo for her paying guests, Ylva would end up in the lower corridor at the back of the building, going along the wall of black and white photographs. St Kilda. There was definitely something about it that struck a chord with her; despite the fact that she had never been to the island. Something about the determination in those sturdy faces from the last communities. Proof against the weather, against what nature might choose to throw at them.

Then she was back in Uig at the end of the line, looking at the old images from the northern Skye mainland. A group of crofters from Uig in the 1800s; keeping a straight face for the slow working camera, squinting eyes from the light and the eternal wind. Fingers chapped with cold. Ylva had been looking at this picture when she had last visited with the American family. Her eyes focused on the melancholic girl with the glossy curls, just off to the side of the group. Her shawl pulled tight around her body, her stare straight at the camera, but her attention, her mind somewhere else completely.

Ylva tapped at the photograph, something in her subconscious trying to break free. "*Jävla!*" she exclaimed, taking a step back from the image. Damn! She stared straight back at the photograph's gaze, and for a moment the image of a Scottish girl long dead seemed to meet her eye. I know you.

"*Are you ok, Ylva?*" Karl appeared by her side as she was flicking through the contents of her shoulder bag. He looked from her to the picture on the wall that had made her jump back. A family photo of a particularly grim looking bunch of Scots. "*Did they give you a fright?*"

"*I've seen her before,*" Ylva said as she drew a piece of paper from her bag.

"*Who?*"

"*The girl; the one to the right with the curly hair. She's clinging onto her shawl.*"

Karl leaned in towards the picture. He could pick out the woman she meant. "*You've seen this picture elsewhere?*"

"*No, the woman.*" The woman in the rain trying to hitch a lift. Ylva unfolded the colour print out Callum McIntosh, the photographer had given her earlier that day, and held it up against the wall beside the picture.

His eyes flickered over to the sheet. "*Wow,*" he let his breath go. The first thing that had struck him when they'd first met Ylva was that she was pretty in an impish kind of way. Here she just looked beautiful. Certainly it was a random picture – she didn't look like the kind of girl who often took a stroll along the beach in a glamorous ball gown. "*Are you some kind of a model?*"

"*What?*" she sounded distracted, glancing across at him. "*No, not me!*" she said, her fingers creeping across her own image to blot it out. "*The girl paddling in the sea.*"

He considered the picture, then back to the black and white photograph. "*Well, they are kind of similar.*"

"*They're the same person.*"

Karl looked over the black and white photograph, catching sight of the date. "*You are joking!*" he laughed. "*This was taken in the 1800s. That girl's been long dead. And this girl,*" he added, tapping Ylva's print out, "*is obviously alive and enjoying the sea. Seriously Ylva, are you trying to talk yourself into having seen a ghost?*"

She smiled weakly, slowly folding her picture. "*I suppose I was.*"

"*It's just a coincidence. Maybe she's a descendant.*"

"*Yes, that's probably it.*"

"*Anyway, that picture raises far more pressing questions.*"

"*Such as?*"

"*Why are you walking on the beach with a ball dress on? It looked very artistic. Yes, now that was haunting.*"

"*Oh, that,*" Ylva waved it off, putting the picture into her bag. "*That was some work I did the other day for the tourist board. They're putting together a new big advertising campaign, and I may or may not been used in the segments for Skye.*"

"*Seriously?*" Karl looked impressed. "*So we might see your photo in the brochures next year?*"

Ylva nodded grimly. "*Unfortunately so.*"

Ylva was usually annoyed when people looked at her as though she was just another tourist. Walking through the Donart Castle car park with Karl, laughing and speaking in Swedish, they definitely stuck out as something very misplaced. But today she didn't care; in fact she didn't even notice when people glanced in their direction; regarding them as another species. If the need for communication had arisen, they would have spoken slowly and loudly, over-pronouncing every word. Smiling politely, drawing up the lines between their differences.

Karl had already lost a lot of his Swedish reservation, without even having to resort to alcohol. He was joking and taking great delight in trying to wind Ylva up the wrong way. "*So you're telling me that there are a lot of ghosts on Skye?*"

"*Oh sure. This is a very mysterious island. There's a lot folklore and legend here. And when the mists come down, it can take on quite a spooky atmosphere.*"

"*And you were just trying to boost the tourist trade by adding another ghost story to the collection.*"

"*Excuse me?*"

"*The curly-haired girl in the photograph.*"

"*I wasn't making that up. You must have seen the resemblance.*"

"*Oh sure, but everyone looks like someone from the past. Admit it: you're wanting to add ghost detective to your website. Bring in a few more paying customers.*"

Ylva laughed out loud. "*I don't know whether I want those kinds of customers.*"

"*You don't actually believe in them, though, do you?*"

"*What, customers?*"

"*No, ghosts.*"

"*No,*" she shook her head. "*No, I don't suppose I really do. Just over reactive imaginations.*"

In the waves of people that walked by – tourists three to one against locals – a man was walking alone, speaking. Ylva had seen him out of the corner of her eye, but her brain didn't register him; and it wasn't until he was almost upon her, touching her elbow that she realised he was speaking to her. Her attention away from Karl, she stared at the man, his facial features not making sense before she focused and recognition hit.

"Dougie." She sounded surprised to see him.

"Ylva," he smiled, a little awkwardly, looking from Ylva to the tall man beside her. "You're taking another one of your tours around?"

"Yes. Dougie, this is Karl, one of my tour groups for this week. Karl, this is one of our local doctors, Dougie."

Karl beamed and offered his hand. "Nice to meet you." It was the first time she'd heard him speak English. He was fluent – all Swedes under a certain age were fluent, brought up on a diet of subtitled American television; English language music and culture – but there was a definite and particular Swedish accent, which sounded painfully clear to Ylva's ear. Having been brought up bilingual, learning English from her Scottish mother, she had never really had a strong Swedish accent, although there was a subtle lilt to her Scottish dialect.

"When I break my legs, I know where to go," Karl continued, joking with Dougie. He turned to Ylva, switching back to Swedish and marking the end of the polite meeting. *"Jag drar tillbaks till bilen. De tre sitter och väntar redan."*

I'll go back to the car. Those three are sitting and waiting already: it was a non-too subtle hint not to stay long talking to Dougie.

"I'd better get off," Ylva said as she lingered behind. "I can't keep them waiting."

"Oh aye. But we're still on for tonight?"

"Tonight?"

"Gaelic?"

"Fan." She swore under her breath, realising there was something she had forgotten whilst Karl had persuaded her to

come to the pub this evening. Stating that he wanted to experience Scottish pub culture, but doubting his sister and cousin would join him; his grandmother certainly wanting an early night; he had played on her sympathy and gained her agreement to accompany him. Ylva glanced up at Dougie and winced. "I'm really sorry, I forgot."

"I take it you've got other plans now."

"They are my paying guests for this week. But my diary is less hectic next week, so I'll manage something then."

"Depending on what my diary is looking like," he tried to make light of it; feeling a little put out that she hadn't remembered. "Don't worry about it. I'll catch you later."

"Thanks, Dougie," Ylva waved to him as she headed back to the minibus, satisfied that everyone was happy with this evening's arrangements. She just had to hear back from Morag that it was ok to sleep over, then she didn't have a worry in the world.

Ylva sat on a rock and smoothed sun block into her arms. A lot of Swedes tanned easily and their skin did not mind the sun. Something about a Swedish-Scottish mix made her sensitive. The sun was unforgiving today, which was both a relief and a curse after the previous two days of rain – so much for forecasts of nothing more than a couple of light showers.

She was perched beside the fairy pools river, the Cullins behind her, looking as though they had been bleached dry by the sun; the air was so bright. This was certainly one of Ylva's favourite places to come, and week-long tour groups rarely escaped without being brought here.

A little further down the river Elena, the youngest, and Ulla Britt, were sitting on canvas chairs working on sketches of the river, illustrating the smoothed rock formations of pools as the mountain river battered downwards. The sound of chatter – Elena's Swedish steadily becoming more confident – was just above the level of running clear water. Stretched out on a rock behind them, so as to not appear in their drawings, lay Harriet, sunbathing. She was the kind of girl who tanned easily, and Ylva was sure she could actually see the skin tone change by the minute. Harriet had not expected to be able to tan during her Scottish journey – sunshine was her main demand usually when booking holidays – and was pleased to find that today she was not obliged to walk or paint if she wasn't inclined, and the weather was actually what she wouldn't have expected for the UK.

Putting the sunblock back into the larger rucksack – containing their lunch and plenty of water – Ylva pulled out the red flag, with three foot extendable shaft, and plunged it into the peaty earth by the heather. So that everyone could find their base and the food; for Karl had continued up the path at a fair pace, saying that he wanted to get to the base of the Waterpipe Gully, the long vertical crack in the forefront mountain ahead. He had promised that he would not attempt to climb it, and Ylva had reminded him to keep to his promise because if he got stuck part way up, she wasn't coming after him. Besides, the waterpipe had a deserved reputation for being a difficult climb and from what Ylva had surmised from previous conversations, Karl didn't rock climb.

Taking only her small knapsack, which contained her camera along with a few other personal items, Ylva left base camp. Dropping down from the earthy bank of heathers onto the bare rock river bank, she walked up with the water edge and peered at her reflection in a side pool for a moment. Jumping across a narrow gully where an inky unknown depth of water crashed in the direction of the next waterfall, she landed on the far side of the river. The majority of visitors tended not to stray to this side of the river; sticking to the main path and not daring to cross the energetic little river. It was good to cross over now and then, to get a different view point of the Cullins, and even the river itself.

Ylva walked up the river for a short distance before stepping up onto the earth, stalking through the heather so that she could take some photographs with a wider shot. It was harder walking where there wasn't a distinct path; the heather acting like water, pulling back at her feet and legs.

She stopped and turned. It was surprising how little air movement there was today, the sun literally baking the atmosphere dry. She squinted in the brightness and stared across the bowl of land to the speck at the base of a patch of forest where the little car park was.

"It's a hot one today."

She hadn't noticed the figure sat on the rock. The rock like an island in a sea of heather, the man a thinking Greek statue. Ylva twisted her torso to glance casually at the source of the voice, and was taken aback to find herself staring unashamedly at a distinctively handsome man. He had what she supposed was the definition of the chiselled jaw; a sculpted face and a body in all the right proportions, from what could be determined from the way his clothes sat on him. Slightly bronzed skin; which wasn't a usual match for his obviously red hair, but it looked well on him. Tousled, slightly unkempt hair that gave him an artistic look. Ylva forgot herself.

The man smiled, amused by her stare. "You must like it up here," he commented. "I've seen you up this way on more than one occasion."

Lord, Ylva thought to herself, how I could just melt into that man.

"And you've decided to come over to the other side today?"

She gave herself a little shake to wake up. She was surprised by just how affected she was by this stranger. "Just to get a different viewpoint."

"Always a wise idea." He nodded as if she had said something particularly profound. "You like the fairy pools?"

Upon mention of the river, Ylva looked back to the water, the turquoise blue glittering, coloured by minerals and rocks; clear mountain water. Gushing forth as it continued ever downwards. "Yes, it's very beautiful."

When she looked back at him, he had already stepped down from his rock, and had waded closer through the heather. "It is; I must agree," he nodded his confirmation. "Have you ever been to the wee burn down there?" He pointed across further away from the main river, to a slight gap in the heather cover where presumably a small tributary stream ran, cut into the earth and not visible from this angle.

"No, I can't say I have."

"I know it's not as long, but it's particularly exquisite. In some ways I think a superior to the main river. There's a seam of blue rock over there; it comes out in the river in an amazing way."

"Really?" She sounded eager.

He flashed her a smile. "Really. Come and take a look." He extended his arm, offering her a hand.

Ylva looked at the hand, following it up along the length of arm, the fabric of the shirt sleeve, and up to his face. His inviting expression, and those charismatic eyes. She found herself reaching out for him without even thinking about it; a man she had only met a few minutes ago; and she didn't even know his name. Something wasn't right.

"No." Her hand dropped suddenly, definite. "I'd better not. I'm here with some people and I shouldn't go wandering off. I should get back to them."

"And you'll let me go and look on my own?" He sounded as though he was pretending to be hurt. He started forward again towards her.

"Today I will." She backed off, heading towards the river. "I have to get back."

"Are you sure, now?" He followed her through the heather.

"Sure. Some other time." Her boots hit the bare rock of the river bank. There was something about the heat that was making her feel giddy. Almost nauseous. Something about his stare that made her lose control of her senses. She didn't understand why she felt as though she was in a panic. Hurrying down a short length of the river, she found her gully and hopped back across. When she looked back to the other side, the nameless man had gone, presumably down the bank to sit by his burn in his intoxicating solitude.

Harriet Ljungström took a deep draft of her pint before speaking for the first time since she had sat down at the pub bench. *"So the live music they're going to be playing here; it's like traditional Scottish?"*

"I think so. It usually is here, but I've not heard of this particular group before."

Ylva, Harriet and Karl were in the beer garden of a small pub in the village of Carbost. Just a minute's walk from the Tallisker whisky distillery, the beer garden overlooked Loch Harport, a sea loch curled around the west side of Skye. The sun was still strong after their day at the fairy pools; the water gently lapping and looking like solid turquoise paint.

Ulla Britt and Elena were a little further down the village, directly outside the whisky distillery. It wasn't the alcohol they were searching for, but the perfect evening light for painting, and set up by the loch edge on the concrete harbour wall, they had a view across the water, eyes flicking from easel to paper.

Karl and Harriet weren't painters, and had wanted to go to a pub instead. Thankfully there was a good pub just up the rising length of village, which often had live music on. Built on the side of the loch, like a corridor of low ceiling-rooms, it was a friendly little place that she had visited a couple of times on non-work related outings with Dougie before.

"Was it traditional Scottish you had playing in the van down here?"

Ylva glanced up at Karl. The CD had arrived in the post that morning; a mixed bag of an album if she were honest, not all of the songs to her taste. She'd only bought it for one of the tracks; the same song the teenagers' band had been playing. A song that she'd been so enthralled by that even suffering the embarrassment of having a juvenile think he had pulled wasn't enough to stop her asking. *"I'm not sure,"* she replied. "*But the singer's Irish. I don't really know so much about that album.*"

"*You seemed to be quite into one of the songs,*" Karl continued. "*Your fingers were playing it on the steering wheel...*"

Ylva pursed her lips: he really had been paying attention. She wasn't used to this kind of scrutiny.

"*I couldn't really follow it; the words were so fast, and maybe a bit weird.*" Karl shrugged. "*I guess my English isn't up to coping with all these strange accents.*"

"*You're telling me,*" Harriet rolled her eyes. "*I thought I was fluent, but I really don't get these Scottish people.*"

"*There was a bit that repeated,*" Karl continued, not really listening to his sister. "*Something about* bonny boys. *That means pretty, doesn't it?*"

It had been during that particular song he'd been watching her. Even now the song was set in the back of her mind; an addictive tune she couldn't shake. She'd find herself unconsciously humming it in quiet moments. "*It's called* Bedlam Boys." Ylva explained, not sure she wanted to get into a long discussion about this. She certainly didn't want to recount her own personal history with the song.

"Bedlam Boys," Harriet repeated, slowly and over-pronounced in an extremely Swedish accent.

"Bedlam *was a mad house in London,*" Ylva added. "*Historically. It's an old folk song, about the nutters living there.*"

"*You know, maybe I did understand some of it,*" Karl said. "*I thought I must have misheard because the bits I got were gruesome. Knives and murder; crushing bones. Wasn't there something about children as well?*"

"*Children's legs being chopped up to make pies for the fairies.*"

"*Jesus,*" Harriet laughed. "*These Brits can be really weird sometimes.*"

"*Well, that's what you get for a country that has a ghost in every village,*" Karl said. "*You've heard that, right?*" He turned to Ylva. *"Although I understand you don't believe in ghosts."*

"No." She gave him a warning glare. She didn't want him making fun of her in front of Harriet, certainly not about the lass from Uig. It was unfortunate he'd been there when she'd seen the similarity of the picture at Donart castle to the girl in the sea in her own photograph.

"I'm still undecided," Harriet started. She stopped as the sound of a few guitar chords strung together came out of the pub. *"Maybe they're going to start soon,"* she said, moving from the picnic bench, the discussion already forgotten. *"I'll go in and check."*

Karl finished his pint. *"Over the last few days, I have come to the conclusion that I really envy your life."*

His statement took her unaware. *"Sorry?"*

"This," he held out his arms. *"It's great. Living in this sparsely populated area. It's beautiful. Running your own business. And it's not like this is a traditional tourist destination, as far as museums and culture go. But it works because of the nature, the geology..."* he drifted off for a moment. *"It's got me thinking. On comparison Sweden's got so many places that could work like this. It's just that we don't market ourselves, have nothing set up. Can you imagine a business like yours on somewhere like Gotland? It'd be fantastic."*

Karl leaned forward across the picnic table, an excited look in his eye. *"It could really work. I know Gotland gets a lot of tourists in July and August, but they're mainly Scandinavians. And a lot of the other months have great weather; although the winter could be a feature in itself. You could really market something at the rest of Europe, America."*

"I suppose," Ylva mused idly. It had been several years since she had last been to Gotland; a Swedish island in the Baltic. She remembered sitting on a sea wall at Visby, the island's main town, dangling her legs over the edge and watching eider ducks bob by on the light waves of the sea. *"There's a lot of scope there."*

"Exactly. I'd love to do something like that."

"Well, why don't you?" Ylva slowly turned her glass – orange juice pure and sober for the designated driver. *"You said yourself you're not exactly in the job of your dreams, working at the library."*

"But I don't know much about the tourist industry," Karl said. *"I know I've studied economics, and I reckon I could deal with being self-employed, running a business. But I wouldn't want to go in to something like that. I'd need to set up with someone who really knew that branch. There'd be a lot of work to do, marketing it abroad."* He paused, watching her closely. *"You should do it."*

"Me?" Ylva laughed out loud. *"I've already got my own business. I certainly don't need two."*

"Just transfer it abroad. Back home to Sweden. Why not? You weren't planning on living here for the rest of your life, were you?"

She suddenly felt as though she was back in careers advice at school. You must think seriously about your future. There's not a lot of jobs out there, so if you don't know what you want, you'll finish with nothing much and life will end up passing you by. So much for careers; Ylva had never managed to get enthused about a career. She had moved because she had wanted to get abroad, to go to Scotland, to try living somewhere else. And she'd stuck since. There had been no master plan, and not only did she not know what she wanted to be doing in five years' time; she did not even think about five years' time. Let it happen when it happened.

"Seriously, I think it's a good idea," Karl continued, growing drunk on his own suggestions. *"We could go into business together. Gotland would really work for a business like yours'. And you'd be back in your native country."*

"I suppose it's a suggestion," Ylva said quietly, feeling distinctly unsettled for the second time that day. She was interrupted as music, definitely live, started to pour out of the pub. *"Look, they've started now. Shall we go in and listen?"*

"*Sure,*" Karl drained his drink. "*But you should think seriously about what I've said. I mean it. It'd be a great way for you to settle back in Sweden.*"

Elena, the youngest of the grandchildren, loitered on the pavement outside the bed and breakfast in Portree the following morning. She looked worried, but brightened when Ylva's van pulled up beside her.

"Ylva, I'm so glad you're here," she burst out in English, her Canadian accent quite apparent. This was the Canadian grandchild, who spoke some Swedish at home, but English was most definitely her mother tongue. She blushed as she realised she'd reverted to her native language. Her grandmother was so keen she'd use this opportunity to improve her Swedish. "*Jag menar, det är bra att du är här nu*," she corrected herself. I mean, it's good that you're here now.

Ylva smiled reassuringly. "*Don't worry; I do speak English if you're more comfortable with that.*"

"*No, it's not that,*" the teenager looked worried again. Perhaps she was wondering if Ylva would tell on her to the grandmother. "*I was just in a bit of a panic. You see, it's Karl.*"

"*Karl?*"

"*He needs to go to hospital; but he says he won't see a doctor. Grandmother is really upset.*"

"*Hospital?*" Ylva looked horrified. What had they been doing for the few hours she'd left them at the bed and breakfast to sleep before the next day of touring? He had been in perfect health when she'd dropped them all here yesterday evening.

"*Come with me,*" Elena grabbed her hand. "*You have to talk to them.*"

The two women, a decade apart, flew through the building, up the stairs and into Karl's room. Ylva didn't know what to make of the situation. Karl was fully dressed, sat on top of a made bed with a blanket over his feet. He pushed on a smile as Ylva appeared, and looked as though he was trying to appear pain-free with increasing difficulty. In opposition sat his sister, Harriet, in a chair by the window, nonchalantly like a teenager with a magazine drooping between her fingers. Ulla-Britt was riled, lecturing Karl that he should take his health more seriously. Silently she was disappointed that this perfect holiday was not to be quite as idealistic as she had hoped. Harriet muttered that if Karl didn't want to see a doctor, it was his problem. If his feet fell off, he deserved it.

"*Elena said that Karl was ill.*" Ylva's statement broke up the family argument. All eyes turned to her.

"*It's nothing. Just a light sprain,*" Karl assured her.

"*It's broken,*" Ulla Britt said.

"*Is this your foot?*" Ylva approached the bed.

"*Well, my ankle,*" Karl started, sitting up a little straighter. This morning was getting stranger and stranger. His ankle hadn't hurt last night when he'd rolled into bed. And now it was red and swollen, and his small bedroom was filled with four women of varying furies, one of which he'd rather have had here under very different circumstances.

"*Can I look?*" She didn't wait for a reply, but lifted the blanket. It was his left ankle, sockless; red and swollen. It didn't look promising. "*What did you do?*"

"*The idiot fell off the doorstep,*" Harriet supplied, rolling her eyes. "*When we got back we nipped out to the pub again. We were trying to sneak quietly in to the bed and breakfast, and this idiot slipped backwards off the doorstep. He didn't even fall on his arse, and even he managed to break his leg.*"

"*I have not broken my leg.*"

"*It might just be a bad sprain,*" Ylva thought out loud.

"*Exactly. So there's no need to panic. I just need a bag of frozen peas.*"

"*You need to see a doctor,*" Ylva concluded. Her word was final. "*My friend works at the surgery just around the corner. I'm sure he'll make time for us this morning. Come on, let's get down to my van and I'll drive you round.*"

Leaving the three women with maps of Portree marking a route around the various craftspeople, pictures and artwork for exploration that morning, Ylva had driven Karl across to the health centre. The receptionist had a free appointment with Dr Douglas MacWhirter, as she had rather pompously called him, and had begrudgingly marked it down in Karl's name, giving up on trying to write his surname and typing Mr Young in the computer.

They slouched down in the waiting room, Karl propping his leg up on the magazine table. "*Maybe it was a good idea to come and check,*" he conceded. "*It is starting to sting a bit.*"

Sting a bit: Ylva looked up at the ceiling. What was that supposed to mean, in man-speak? He was in bloody agony? "*Do you want me to come in with you?*"

"*No, I'll be fine.*"

Dougie put his head through the door. "Mr Young?"

Karl put his hand up.

Dougie looked surprised. He looked from Ylva to Karl and back to Ylva. "Ylva, is everything all right? You're here with... Mr Young?" He didn't sound quite convinced by the name. But he recognised the man from Donart Castle car park where he had seen the two of them chattering like old friends.

"I'm not really Mr Young," Karl said as he stood up on his right leg. "It was easier than to explain the spelling."

"We think he might have sprained his ankle." Ylva added.

"Oh right, let me help you there," Dougie started forward to take Karl's arm and give him a bit of support as they hobbled back to his room.

Ylva sank back in to her chair. So much for her plans of taking a boat round into the inner loch at the heart of the Cullin mountains and hiking round the shore line. It didn't look as though there'd be anymore walks on this holiday. Whether it was a sprain or a break, Karl was going to have to keep the weight off his ankle for a few days at the very least. She picked up one of the trashy magazines common to waiting rooms and flicked through to kill the time.

When Dougie and Karl returned ten minutes later, they both looked almost embarrassed. Ylva stood up spritely.

"I don't think it's broken. Just a bad sprain," Dougie said, "But I want you to go to the hospital to check it."

Karl looked a little sheepish, as if this was a slight on his male maturity. "I think it's an overreaction."

"It's not a problem," Ylva assured him. "I'll send Ulla-Britt a text message and then I'll drive you there."

He wouldn't look her in the eye out to the van.

In fact, thinking back over the afternoon, Karl had behaved strangely. Ylva had put it down to injured male pride – not wanting anyone to witness him in such a vulnerable state. The hospital confirmed what Dougie had said – the ankle was not broken. Which was lucky for Karl, because ankle breaks could be nasty things to try and fix.

She drove him back to the bed and breakfast; Karl had said that he only wanted to sleep. He didn't feel particularly hungry, and didn't want company; virtually chasing her from the guest house's door with his crutch-on-loan from the hospital. Ylva had called Ulla-Britt and arranged to meet the three women in town. They'd gone for a drive up the north of the island to pass by some of the geological features – the Old Man of Storr, Kilt Rock and the Quiraing. They'd returned to Portree for a prompt evening meal, in dampened spirits, and separated early. It had been a let down of a day and Ylva hadn't felt like talking: rather than crashing at Morag's another night, she had driven back to Broadford despite the extra miles it would cost her.

The following morning she didn't try to arrive too early, thinking that they wouldn't be rushing in the hopes of a full and busy day sightseeing now that Karl's foot was out of action. Ylva spent the drive over to Portree trying to work out a good schedule for someone who essentially wouldn't be walking for the rest of the holiday. He had been subdued yesterday, and she didn't want him to feel that he was spoiling the remainder of the trip for everyone else.

Alison Drummond, the owner of the bed and breakfast, was in the front hallway looking through the post when Ylva stepped in. "Morning, Alison," she said. "Are they still having breakfast?"

Alison, a sixty-something ex-Orkney resident looked a little confused as Ylva leant into the breakfast room in search of her guests. "They had breakfast hours ago. They had to get away prompt."

"Sorry?"

"Well, the train was going pretty early and they had a taxi booked." Alison stopped, watching Ylva's reaction. "Did they not have chance to tell you? To be fair, they barely had chance to tell me. It was all very sudden. Although they paid for the whole week as booked, so I can hardly complain, I suppose."

"They've left Skye?" Ylva asked, as if she was slow on the uptake.

Alison nodded. "Aye."

"They've gone home?"

"Away back to Norway or wherever it was they were from. Did they not tell you at all?"

She felt sick. The same sensation as walking in to a room where everyone was laughing and she wasn't let in on the joke. Or walking into a room and the conversion suddenly stops. "There were only two more days to go. I know Karl had twisted his ankle, but I was prepared to work around that."

"That's probably it. He had sprained his ankle. They probably just wanted to get away as soon as possible. Ach, don't take it to heart. Different people have different ways about them. And they were foreigners."

Just like me, Ylva thought silently. Alison was one of the few people who treated her like a proper local. To the point that she genuinely appeared to forget that Ylva did actually come from another country.

"You've been paid for your work, though?"

"Oh yes," she replied numbly. "I've been paid. I'd better be off then."

"Be seeing you, girl," Alison called after her. "And don't forget to give me a ring if you get any more groups wanting to book accommodation."

It was a cold morning, the wind moving briskly up the road. Ylva stood and stared blankly down the length of pavement. What had happened? She had thought they were enjoying their trip in Scotland. Okay, Karl had sprained his ankle, but she could have still shown them things without needing to go hiking. At the very least she could have driven them to the train station. She had thought she and Karl were getting along well. She had thought. Ylva took her mobile phone out of her pocket and unlocked it. She didn't know what to think. She tried Karl's number, but was told that the phone was switched off. She sent a quick text message: *Vad har hänt? Är allt bra?* What's happened? Is everything ok? She rang Ulla-Britt's number, which rang for an eternity before going to answer phone. She left a message. Harriet's number rang twice then an automated voice told her that the person she was trying to call was busy. Ylva held the phone away from her. If she was paranoid, she might think they were avoiding her.

On the drive back to Broadford – a suitably wasted trip and litres of needlessly burned petrol – she went over the possibilities. Perhaps there had been a death or a problem in the family and they needed to get back to Sweden as soon as possible. It may have nothing whatsoever to do with Karl's ankle. Alison had said that they had been in a rush – no time to call Ylva and apologise that they had to break off the trip suddenly. But it was such strange behaviour, and a sudden change of heart. They had been getting along extremely well – at least Ylva had thought so.

She tried to call them again when she got home. Karl's mobile was not on, and neither was Ulla-Britt's. Harriet's flicked over to the busy message after one ring. She was being shunned. And she had no idea why.

Ylva and Morag sat on the bench like two little girls comparing their shoes. Morag's heels were a good inch longer than Ylva's; bright red patent shoes that looked like they were straight out of a bordello in Oz. Morag had patted her bag. I look cute in these, she'd told Ylva, but I've got my plimsolls in here for when the dancing gets going.

Ylva had blockier heels on and was hoping her feet wouldn't ache too much as she hadn't brought any alternative footwear. She didn't want to be dancing in her bare feet either as the risk of sticky spilt alcohol residues and the odd broken glass grew as the night went on.

They were at the hotel in Sligachan – a little place with a famous stone bridge; half way between Portree and Broadford as the crow might fly. There was a big caeidh on for the night and people from all over the island were expected. The car park was full, as were the verges and footpaths, side roads and every available section of level ground. There was a good folk band playing, a loudspeaker system that would allow dancing in the garden as well as the main hall – cleared of the furniture – and a restaurant area handed over for dancing.

Morag grinned and nudged Ylva with her shoulder.

"Hey, what was that for?" Ylva glanced over. "You're looking particularly cheerful."

"I know."

"Oh, come on then, share it; spit it out." She didn't mean to sound quite as bitter as she did, but she was still put out from her Swedish tour party abandoning her without a word. Answer phone messages, texts and emails were unanswered. She definitely wasn't being paranoid, three days after the event. She was being intentionally ignored. She didn't know why, and she couldn't think of anything she had done wrong. It left a horrible taste.

"I might have met someone," Morag confessed.

"Met someone? You mean like a man?"

"Oh yes. Well, not so much met, 'cause I've known him for years. But getting to know him better, if you know what I mean."

"And do I know him?"

"You might."

Ylva mouthed the name Colm.

Morag shook her head. "Oh no, that's all dead and buried. You've got to move on from stuff that'll go nowhere. This is much more positive."

"And are you going to tell me who it is?"

She pretended to think it over, then shook her head. "Not yet. I don't want to jinx it."

I wish I had something to be cheerful about, Ylva thought. A bout of wallowing self-pity started to swell from the depths. Oh, Scandinavian depression and brooding. Pondering over the meaning of life and trying to remember what the sun looked like.

"You lasses aren't planning on dancing in those, are you?"

Colm stood in front of them, hands hooked into the pockets of his jeans as if he were about to break out into a line dance at any moment. Ylva glanced up at his warm crinkled face. He seemed very cheery as well tonight – no more cat burnings on his beach and a wee dram before he headed out for a night's social in Sligachan.

"I've got my shoes for later," Morag said, taking her plimsolls out of her handbag for a brief second as if she was airing stolen goods. "But in the meantime, I can't not use these shoes. Incredibly impracticable, but I'll look oh so elegant."

The loudspeaker crackled into life. A few notes of a violin rang through the air, warm, earthy vibrations. A cough, then the leader of the group spoke. "Good evening, ladies and gents. And welcome to our caelidh. We're in for a grand old night. We'll start off with something nice and easy to get you going before the business of the night kicks off. Take your partners please, and we'll have a round of the Gay Gordons."

Colm smiled, and casually offered his hand to Morag. "Shall we take them out for a spin before you're over the limit?"

"Colm!" Morag shrieked. "I hope you're not suggesting I'm a common drunk." She accepted his hand anyway.

Ylva watched them walk off into the gathering of dancers, expectant for the first of the caelidh dancers. She propped her chin up on her hands and gazed off into the middle distance. She wasn't sure that she should have come – she came because she had promised and because Morag had dragged her here. But she wasn't in the right mood. She shivered as a cool breeze came through the half-open window behind her. It would be a blessing as the evening went on and the body temperature rose, but now, sitting in a strappy sun dress and open-toed sandals, she wasn't dressed for warmth. Ylva checked her watch and rolled her eyes. There was still hours to go before she could respectfully leave.

The Gay Gordons, a rather tame, lolling dance, started up. The couples trotted neatly along in rows, the music steady and predictable. The pace would pick up in the evening, the fiddle music furious so that the notes would almost trip over one another in an eagerness to get on with the tune. Everything had to start somewhere.

She stood up, considering a trip to the bar, when she saw a familiar figure walking towards her. A teenager, almost ready to stretch out and fill a man's body and mind, but still a couple of years off maturity. Where had she seen him before?

"Hey, Yullvay," he greeted her, offering a new variation on her name that she actually hadn't heard before – which was some achievement considering how often people struggled with her name.

This was the boy who had emailed her the lyrics to that folk song she'd liked. Bedlam Boys. The one she'd found a better version of, professionally recorded. He was a local teenager in a local band that would entertain for a few weeks. Full of big ideas of himself. Ylva smiled weakly. She didn't need this.

"It's Chris," he reminded her. "You enjoying your Boys of Bedlam?"

"Sure," she nodded. She didn't quite have the heart to tell him she'd found a recording that really did the song justice.

"And you're here to sample some more of our Scottish culture?"

Jesus, did he have to be so condescending? The old cliché was that teenagers reckoned they knew everything, and everyone past twenty-five knew nothing; but really, did he have to play up to it so much? "I'm just here to catch up with a few friends."

"Really?" He looked a little surprised by this, his body stance altering a little. "So you, like, live round here?"

"On Skye."

"Yes, that's what I meant."

Ylva glanced across at him. Did he think she'd been asking a question? On Skye? As if she wasn't sure where she was. She needed a drink – she was growing particularly irritated and defensive.

"Well," he started, a little awkwardly for the first time. Moving as if to ask her to dance, then changing his mind or losing his courage, and mentally running away. "I'm here to see my own friends. I'll maybe see you around tonight."

Everything was messed up. She had somehow offended her Swedish tour group without realising it and now the local school boys were sniffing around as if she was something worth a second glance. She was twenty-eight: this was not the direction her life was supposed to be progressing in.

"Have you checked that he's over sixteen?"

She jumped at the sound of a voice so close and unexpected. Her irritation was soon back. "Oh, sod off, Dougie."

"Come on, Ylva." He slung an arm around her shoulder. His breath had a touch of whisky to it. A little tipsy, but not drunk. Still steady on his feet and able to walk in a straight line. Very sure of what he was saying. "I'm only jesting with you. But that lad seems very taken with you. I suppose this is what happens when mysterious Scandinavian women come up to you asking for your email and your song lyrics. That's how it always starts."

"You all right today, Dougie?"

"I'm grand. Because it's the weekend."

"It always helps."

"Your Swedes get away home all right?"

She tensed up. Most people didn't know the details of her diary and her tour groups. No one apart from Alison had spoken to her about the abrupt departure of her paying guests. She didn't want anyone to know, feeling as though it was a mark of shame against her name. She lowered her eyes. "They went home early."

"Early? You mean they cut the tour short? Well, maybe he didn't fancy it with a sprained ankle. What can I say: no stamina."

Ylva suddenly felt close to tears. "Did they say anything to you?"

"To me?"

She twisted to look Dougie in the eye. "When I brought Karl in to see you. Did he say anything?"

"Well, he spoke, but nothing about anything in particular." Dougie's brow creased in concern a little, the joke gone. "What's happened?"

"They just packed their bags and left early next morning," Ylva quietly confided in him. "I found out when I got to the B&B and Alison said they'd left. I haven't been able to get in touch with them."

"They didn't say anything to you?"

She shook her head.

"Maybe it's just with the travelling…"

"Travelling to Sweden doesn't take that long," she interrupted him. "I keep going over the week in my mind again and again, trying to think of what I might have done and I can't think of anything. And I come up with nothing. I just don't understand it."

"Maybe they've had a family drama and they had to dash," Dougie offered feebly. "People are funny. It's hard to know what's going on in other people's minds…"

"I wish I knew." Ylva stared out into the dancers. A dance had just finished, and the band leader was explaining the next dance to commence. It was a fast one, with a lot of circles and spinning; a couple of partner changes along the way.

"This evening is for fun," Dougie concluded as best he could, letting his hand drop down her arm to take her hand. "Come on, you can't come to a caelidh and not dance." He pulled her round to face him quite decisively, a proper lead, and set his hand on her waist. "Care to dance?"

"I'll think about it."

"No, no, no," he scolded, walking her to the dancing. "Thinking is not for tonight."

The dance wasn't too difficult – consisting mainly of spinning around – just as long as you span in the same direction as the other couples in the interchanging larger circle. It could lead to a lot of collisions, especially later in the nightly proceedings, when people's judgement was fuzzy from the alcohol. Determination to get the dance right lessened by laughter.

Ylva felt as though she was standing on the edge of a well-known joke; not understanding because she'd arrived too late or simply didn't belong. People were laughing and talking despite the fact that their heads would soon be spinning. Dougie was grinning at her as if he knew something she didn't. Plotting a prank. He gripped her tighter by the waist and spun faster. "Dougie!" Ylva screeched, her arms going rigid, fingers sinking into his arms like claws. If he let go of her now, the force would fling her up over the Cullins.

"And everyone change partners."

She was catapulted into the fray, suddenly released, staggering like a drunk. Her next partner moved fluidly through the dance, catching her as she turned around. Arms coming down to encase her. Ylva raised her eyes and felt her breath evaporate from her body. Music pounded in her brain; people crowded in on her, everyone blind to her apart from the man who now held her. Time seemed to slow.

The stranger smiled back at her gaze of shock. "You disappointed me the other day," he told her as he spun her around. "You should have come with me to the burn."

Ylva was forgetting herself, drowning in the stare of his eyes. He was the definition of intoxicating. And this wasn't normal behaviour for Ylva, to be so suddenly and abruptly the weak female swooning for a good-looking man. It was frightening how the effect was immediate. Their first meeting up by the fairy pools at the foot of the Cullins had been short. An introduction, formal, keeping a certain distance. Now she was entwined in this man's arms and she felt as though she never would; never could break free. It didn't even matter or register. "*Borde jag?*"

He broke into a flashing, winning broad grin. Ylva blushed as she realised she'd gone into a daydream, switched off and reverted to her native language.

"So you're not a local?"

"It's all relative," she said defensively. "Besides, are you? I've only seen you the once before."

"Oh, I'm more local than the locals themselves, don't you know?" he laughed. "But I think you must live nearby. I've seen you too often for you to be a passing tourist."

"I might do," she said. She wanted to ask where he lived. But it was too forward and the words stuck in her throat.

"You want to get yourself down to that burn," he advised her. "It's the most beautiful thing you'll ever see in this life."

"I'll try next time I'm up there."

He nodded. "I'll hold you to it."

Hold me to what? And the partners were changing, the voice on the loudspeaker demanding people move on. The crowds swelled as Ylva was released. She found herself with Dougie again, feet back on the ground.

"Who was that you were chatting with?"

Ylva looked over her shoulder, barely noticing Dougie, looking for the stranger in the dancers, but he had melded into the crowds. She didn't even know his name. She gripped Dougie's arms for support, still feeling giddy from the surprise meeting. Looking back, him pretending not to be bothered she was virtually blind to his company, she shrugged, and pretended she hadn't just met the most beautiful man on earth. "Just a dance partner."

Dougie looked at her quizzically. "Looked like quite a conversation going on."

"Well, I've bumped into him before, out walking."

"Oh aye?"

The music came to a stop and there was clapping and cheering. Red faces from exertion. Smiling. Heavy breathing. People pulling apart, suddenly embarrassed that they'd clung so tightly during the rush. Ylva stepped back but Dougie still had hold of one of her arms.

"You and me should go out walking sometime. It's been a while now."

Ylva thought it over. "It has. We'll go up the Old Man next time I'm up your way."

"And when will that be?"

"Oh, I don't know." She shrugged. "Anyway, there's that stupid exhibition soon in a few weeks and you said you'd come with me for moral support."

"I did?"

"Well, I haven't asked you yet, but I already answered on your behalf." Ylva grinned. "The Scottish tourist board. You know they signed me up to help promote Skye?"

"Oh, of course," he nodded as they walked to the side of the room. "They had you walking along the beach like a mad woman."

Ylva rolled her eyes. "Yes, Dougie. That'd be the one."

She had never been comfortable seeing photographs of herself hung on the wall or placed on bookshelves in her family home. It was still a little out of character that she'd gone so public in agreeing to feature in a major advertising campaign. Seeing her image in the glossy shots really drove the reality home. It was particularly distressing to discover they'd had long banners of the photographs printed, which were now hung like flags on all the street lamps in the square in Portree. On her way to the central tourist office, where the exhibition opening was to be held, Ylva had come to the square and was horrified to meet her own stare on a flapping banner, the wind rippling over the fabric in a mimic of the depicted sea tide and the way the salty breeze had moved through her hair. It was an ethereal, poetic image, but she didn't like to see herself tangled up in the effect.

Ylva Johansson – local tour guide on Skye: was the subtitle at the bottom of her own particular advertising shot. It smacked of fraud. It was a month now since her party of Swedes had mysteriously walked out on her. She had never managed to get in touch with them, despite telephone calls, messages and emails, she was effectively blanked out. Regardless of the fact that she could think of nothing she had done which could have caused such a reaction, she still worried that it was a sign she was incompetent. As if they had discovered some great secret that she was a mere pretender. There was something about her that made people want to leave. Since that week, she had taken several groups out on various tours. No one had walked out in disgust, and everyone seemed reasonably satisfied. But Ylva was on her guard, paranoid of how things could be misinterpreted, and fussed around her visitors, worried over drops of rain and pandered to every request.

Dougie was waiting in light drizzle outside the tourist information office. Shrunk into his coat against the damp chill. He looked a little awkward, which stuck out because Dougie usually looked as though he always meant to be where he was. He glanced down the street and visibly brightened when he saw Ylva approaching. "Ylva!"

"Yeah," she groaned, second-guessing him. "Sorry I'm late."

"I think they're already had some speeches."

Ylva raised her eyes to the darkening skies. "Thank god I'm as late as I am, then."

"If you were planning on being late, you could have let me in on the arrangements. I needn't have stood out here in the drizzle like a sad case."

"It wasn't so much planned as it just happened this way," Ylva told him. "Let's go in and get this over with."

Considering it was a small, local exhibition for a series of adverts that wouldn't even be used in this area, there were a surprising number of people present Ylva didn't recognise. Skye's population was over 9,000, and whilst you could never get to know each individual by name, after a few years you got to know a lot of the faces – particularly within the tourist industry – especially if you travelled about on the island as much as Ylva did. Perhaps a lot of people from the mainland had come across for the grand opening – but it was hardly a grand opening premiere, and a few large, poster-sized images and a collection of short videos on repeat were hardly exhibition-of-the-year material. But then Skye was changing, the island of late becoming more populated and diversified, with hi-tech business, a Gaelic college and an arts presence. There were more people and perhaps more of the modern, adaptable lifestyle than Ylva's sometimes rose-tinted view of the island would like to admit.

Helena, the tourist information office of Broadford personified, stood with a bunch of colleagues, cronies, each with a glass of cheap wine. She saw Ylva as soon as she walked through the door, and raised her glass. "Great snaps, Il-va!"

Dougie and Ylva loitered at the door, drizzle-damp hair as if it were still drying from the shower. Faced with a wall of groups and chatter. "This all looks very well to do," Dougie commented.

"Jesus," Ylva muttered under her breath. "I don't know what we're doing here."

Dougie laughed. "I know we're a pair of scruffs, but we won't bring the tone down that much."

"Speak for yourself."

They wove around the small groups of intelligent conversation to the photographs displayed on the walls. Maired in Donart Castle gardens in medieval dress – it sounded like a twee concept but the picture had been well-planned. It made Maired look like a flicker of a moment, a cross-over of two times, before she walked back into the past. Next up was Ylva on the beach at Broadford, looking back over her shoulder in the start of movement to turn and face the viewer. The sea breeze blew, rippling through the skirts of her dress, her hair, blowing through the shawl like a flag. Beside it was a similar photograph where she had turned around, an odd glimmer of a smile in the corner of her mouth.

"These are really good," Dougie spoke quietly. "They look like stills from a film."

"The photographer was really good," Ylva said. "Leonard was saying he's done a lot of media work in the last few years – for publishers and all sorts."

"Really good," Dougie repeated as if she hadn't understood him the first time. He was still staring at the line of Ylvas on the wall.

"Come on," she tugged at his arm. "Let's go look at the videos."

In a darkened room usually reversed for the standard locally made intro-to-Skye video to fill twenty minutes of passing tourists' time, they were now showing the finalised adverts. The seats were all full, and people crowded in to watch. Dougie and Ylva had to stand at the archway, leaning in to get a view. They were coming to the end of an advert with Maired – this time in contemporary clothing – standing outside of Donart Castle, welcoming visitors to Skye. A moment of black for the change over, then the wind whistled across the steep hills, and they were hiking in the Quiraing with Ylva. She was chattering away about the geology of the area, walking on the green expanse of the table and turning around. Not so glamorous this time in her jeans, hiking boots and waterproof jacket; brightly coloured woollen hat pulled over her loose hair to stop it blowing around like flames. Ylva cringed as her eyes goggled out of the screen back at her as she babbled on about the Quiraing.

"Jesus, she's keen," someone whispered to their neighbour in the dark.

"She's the one in the beach pictures."

"Seriously?"

"Yes."

"Let's get a tour booked!"

Ylva stepped away from the archway, feeling acutely embarrassed. She hadn't fully considered the kind of comments she would have to take having put herself up for this advertising campaign, and it wasn't the type of attention she wanted. Dougie didn't notice her physically step back – he probably hadn't even heard the unseen men – and was single-mindedly watching the video.

Someone touched her arm. She turned.

"Yuellva," Leonard, the man from the Scottish tourist board in charge of this campaign, smiled at her. "I was hoping you were here. I was beginning to worry when I couldn't see you at the start."

"I was a wee bit late," she admitted.

"Not to worry. I'm glad you could join us. Could we borrow you for a few minutes? We'd like to get a few pictures now that we're got all of our local tourist workers together in one place."

"Sure." She glanced back at Dougie, who was still oblivious to her. She'd pick him back up out of the crowds later. "Is Callum here today?" she asked after the photographer.

"No, unfortunately not," Leonard said. "He wanted to – this is actually our first opening in one of the local areas – in situ, to say. But family things came up and he had to head home. I keep meaning to tell you, by the way, we'll send over some prints eventually when we get sorted round. You might want to send one over to your family – let them see what you're up to. It's not every day you get to have a Callum MacIntosh portrait done."

"No, I don't suppose it is," Ylva responded, her voice a little weak. Leonard made Callum sound like a high society photographer – reserved only for celebrities and the rich. He had seemed far too down to earth for such a vacuous profession.

Maired grinned and gave a little wave as Ylva and Leonard approached the group of willing – if slightly unorthodox at times – models for the latest tourist campaign. "Eelva," she said, "I was worried you weren't going to come. "I didn't want to be the only woman from the Skye group here." She lowered her voice as Ylva stepped into the formation beside her for the photo. "You don't think my pictures look silly, do you?"

"What do you mean? The pictures are really well done."

"Aye, I know. But wandering around in a medieval dress…"

"Was it your idea?"

Maired shook her head.

"It looks really good, don't worry. It looks like a shot from a film."

"There is that kind of look to them," Maired agreed, as they turned to face the camera. "And the ones with you look fantastic," she added. "Everyone'll be wanting to take a tour with Eelva Johansson."

Everyone but the Swedes, Ylva thought, forcing a smile for the camera. One more picture and it would all be over.

Pictures and pleasantries complete, the small group dispersed back into the crowd for the rest of the evening. Ylva filtered out to the edge, going to the front of the shop to stare out of the glass doors onto Portree. Dusk was falling heavy;

the drizzle had thickened off into mist, giving the street a slightly eerie look as the streetlamps began to light up. Outside the newsagent closed for the night stood a young woman, in a long dress, a shawl of tartan draped around her shoulders. Her dark brown curls were knotted and unbrushed, tumbling thoughtlessly around her face.

Ylva leaned forward, recognising her as the woman Callum had caught paddling in the sea during the photo shoot. The woman in the photograph in Donart castle – at least a very close resemblance. Someone she had once seen hitchhiking out of Uig. And here she was again, as if Ylva was the object of her stalking obsession. She would have to go and speak to the girl, to prove to herself that she wasn't going mad, and that not only did this woman exist, but she was real.

Pushing open the door, she left the busy, warm environment of the tourist office and entered the damp evening air. Mist swelled around the buildings of Portree. Visibility was reasonable. She half-expected the woman to vanish like a mirage as she left the building, but she was still outside the newsagent, and now staring at Ylva.

Ylva didn't quite know what to do at this point. Despite the coincidences and random meetings, they were still strangers who had never knowingly come in to contact. She raised her hand a little, opened her mouth to say something. The woman across the road shrugged a little, then abruptly ran across the road to a snicket between two buildings.

"Wait!" Ylva sprinted after the stranger, skidding at the corner where the snicket, a steep length of steps, went down to the little harbour. Usually seen featuring on postcards and boxes of fudge, the brightly painted houses lit up by the summer, it was now a foreboding place, as if on the edge of the earth, the sea water lapping out into the nothingness that was hidden by the mist.

The girl was already at the bottom of the steps. As she ran, Ylva realised that not only was she carrying a sturdy pair of boots in one hand, laces knotted together, but that the girl was running bare foot.

Ylva jogged down the steps, wondering if this girl was from a local care home, a little simple perhaps. It was cold and damp and people these days didn't have the feet for walking barefoot over rock, concrete and tarmac long distance for the simple reason that modern footwear made feet soft and supple, with no use for the thickening of skin into hard layers like a self-grown pair of shoes.

Walking brusquely along the harbour wall, she watched the girl cautiously. She had stopped at the end of the harbour and was looking down into the water as if she was thinking of jumping. Ylva halted a good ten metres away, suddenly feeling self conscious. She didn't really know what to say.

The girl took a sharp intake of breath, turned and faced Ylva. She smiled shyly and tilted her head slightly.

Something was wrong. Ylva felt the chill creep through her body. "Who are you?" she asked the girl. She didn't get an answer. "What's your name?"

The girl smiled again. "Maud."

"Maud?" That was a particularly old-fashioned name for the girl's generation. She only looked as though she was in her early twenties.

The girl started to walk to her, feet padding over the rough surface of the ground.

"What's going on? Why do you keep following me?"

The girl picked up speed. "My name is Maud."

"I know that; you just said."

Suddenly she was running again, her boots swinging by her side. She rushed at Ylva, whipping up beside her and away. Ylva felt the turbulence of moving, as if the air filtered through her very bones. She twisted around on her heel, but the girl was gone. She turned around a full 360 degrees, surveying the area but she was most definitely alone on the harbour front. If she hadn't heard Maud's voice, she would have been sure she had imagined the entire episode.

Ylva stood up and watched the little boy sulking by the frothy edge of the sea. She decided she would have to make one last effort to get in touch with her Swedes. The little boy was sulking because he was only six years old; his brother had found the footprints; and because sometimes, at that age, you simply needed to sulk. But somewhere inside she was worrying that this sulk was all her fault. That had she been a competent tour guide, the boy would never have become huffy. Because there were things she was doing wrong. Things she knew nothing about.

It was an afternoon tour – a few short hours. These kinds of tours were good to fill in the gaps, bulk up her summer earnings and do a few odd little bits, meet some people who perhaps wouldn't usually go on tours. But for a few hours they didn't want to plan or think, and were happy to pay for someone who knew where everything was and the quickest way to get there. This particular family, an English group from Sussex, consisted of the standard mother and father and two little boys – one nine, one six. Bowing out to the needs of their children, they'd asked if there was any way to incorporate dinosaurs into an afternoon on Skye. Of course there was, said Ylva. There are dinosaur footprints to the north of Skye. The geology is particularly fascinating – although it took a lot of imagination and colour-me-in worksheets to keep little boys happy. The dinosaur footprints in question were forever imprinted in rock at the side of a little beach on the north-east coast. Covered over in slime and wreaths of seaweed, it took a little time to locate them – which was part of the adventure – but even when they'd cleaned the sea refuse away, they were never as exciting as people hoped. Still, the little boys had appeared to be reasonably impressed, especially after the youngest got over his grumpiness.

The following day found her with a couple of hours to kill before she needed to be in Portree for another unconstructive language exchange session. She really needed to wipe out the if and the doubt and call Sweden again. She had to settle her mind and find out what had happened. She had found Karl's home telephone number through a combination of the telephone directory online and the process of deduction. She had called a couple of times before, but he had not answered. As the weeks passed her determination had waned. It had been easier to continue in ignorance than face up to the possibility that she might have a deluded self-image.

She couldn't go on like this. Ylva dialled the number and listened to the ring tone.

"Hallo. Ljungström."

It was Karl. She felt something catch in the back of her throat. *"Karl,"* she started, in Swedish. *"This is Ylva Johansson. I was your tour guide on Skye."*

There was a sharp intake of breath on the other end of the line.

"Don't hang up," she blurted out in a panic. *"I'm not calling you to cause you grief. I'm just concerned. You all left so abruptly and without any message. I've been trying to get in touch to find out what was wrong."*

"I know."

Ylva bit her tongue in irritation. Then why haven't you replied? You're in another country now; far, far away from having to deal with me. *"I can understand that you might have wanted to cut the trip short, with your sprained ankle, but why didn't you get in touch and let me know? You all had my mobile number."*

"It wasn't because of that," Karl said. He sounded a little weary, as if he didn't really want to have this discussion with her. *"I suppose we just didn't want to cause a scene."*

"Cause a scene?"

"You know, start an argument with you. It just seemed easier..."

"You didn't want an argument?" She was trying her best to keep her voice level. But she felt exasperated by this

culmination of avoiding the issue. *"So you just did a midnight flit?"*

"We did leave early in the morning."

"Can you be anymore Swedish?"

"Swedish?" There was laughter in his voice – confusion. *"What do you mean by that? You're Swedish as well."*

Ylva glared out of the window. He knew what *typisk svensk* was. Typically Swedish. Swedes had a reputation for being standoffish, keen to avoid confrontation. It infuriated her, and her father always told her that it was just her mother coming out in her. She ought to relax and not rock the boat. Be adaptable to change and accept the way things went. It only made her all the more angry.

"Well, I'm far across the sea in another country, so you needn't worry about me getting aggressive. I can't hit you all the way from Scotland. Could you please just tell me what happened? I've been worrying all this time that I did something wrong."

"But you don't need me to tell you what you did. You know it already. That's part of the reason why we didn't call you."

"You're speaking in riddles."

"You know how you run your business."

"And what exactly is that supposed to mean?"

Karl grew silent for a moment. *"I don't really know how to say all of this. Maybe you think the way you work is ok, and that's your decision. I don't think it's right, but I don't want to get involved. You don't need to worry. We're not going to report you."*

"Report me?"

"I was really disappointed when we left Skye. I actually thought I'd found a good idea: something to do with my life that wasn't just filling in at the library and wasting away. I'd got all these plans, running my own business and living on Gotland. You and me over there. We could have really made a go of it."

"What are you talking about? We hadn't made any arrangements to go into business together."

"But we could have. It was a really solid idea. And I thought we'd clicked. I really got along with you that week."

"I thought we were all getting along well," Ylva said quietly. *"Which was why I was so surprised when you left the way you did."*

"I don't take big risks. Not like that. I couldn't run a business the way you do."

This was getting beyond irritating. *"Look, if you're going to accuse me of some unprofessional behaviour, I think you should just spit it out rather than dancing around the issue."*

She could feel him step back from her, mentally startled by the aggression. He didn't like confrontation.

"You're not insured. I don't know where you stand legally, but anyway..."

"Excuse me?"

"And, okay, I know my ankle wasn't your fault, but I understand you've had a few accidents. A couple of broken ankles and legs. You push people beyond what they're capable of and don't take due care and attention..."

"What the hell are you talking about?" Ylva shouted into the phone. Her hand was balled up into a fist. How dare he talk such nonsense. *"What kind of a person do you think I am? Of course I'm bloody insured. Do you think I'd still be operating after all this time without insurance? And no one has ever had a broken bone whilst on holiday with me. Ever."*

"But…"

"How dare you spout such crap about me without any evidence? And no evidence can exist because it's all lies."

"But he told me all of this," Karl sounded subdued.

"He told you this?" Ylva snapped. *"And just who is he supposed to be?"*

"On our last day, when you took me to get my ankle looked at."

"At the hospital? You mean someone at the hospital told you I was unprofessional and a liability?" Who could it have been? A competitor? There were other tour guides and organisations on Skye, but if there was this kind of back

handed behaviour going on, Ylva had kept out of it quite neatly up until now.

"*No, before then. The little place we first went to. I saw the doctor. He said he thought it was just a sprain but that we ought to go to the hospital to get an x-ray just in case. He told me that this had happened a few times with you. People had broken bones, so you were lucky to get away with a sprain this time. We had to be careful because you weren't insured.*"

She felt nauseous. "*A doctor told you this?*"

"*This doctor you took me to. I think you know him quite well. I remember we bumped into him at that castle earlier.*"

"*You don't mean Dougie, do you?*"

"*Dougie?*"

"*Dr Douglas MacWhirter.*"

"*Yes, that's the one.*"

Ylva squeezed her eyes shut tightly. This didn't make any sense. Dougie was supposed to be her friend. "*I don't see why he would make up lies like that about me.*"

"*Neither do I,*" Karl admitted. "*But he was quite adamant you were a liability.*" He paused, perhaps feeling guilty, or at the very least not quite so certain in his condemnation of her. "*But look at it from my point of view, Ylva,*" he pleaded. "*The man's a doctor. What possible reason could he have had for lying about something like that?*"

Dougie MacWhirter sat at a small round table in the bar room. There was an almost full pint in front of him. He wasn't paying that much attention to the movement of people in the pub, the new entrances and the people leaving. He was talking to a retired fisherman who was propping up the bar. He didn't see Ylva enter the pub, and was a little surprised when his line of sight shifted and she was suddenly stood on the other side of the table from him. Five minutes before they had arranged to meet for their language exchange.

"Ylva!" he greeted her merrily. "Pull up a chair."

Ylva picked up his pint and threw it in his face. Dougie gasped, reeling back in his chair as the short-lived tidal alcoholic wave splashed over him, drenching his hair and his face. The fisherman drew the air in sharply between his teeth. The pub held its breath, conversations close by faltering abruptly at the break out of drama.

"*Ditt jävla kräk.*" Ylva said, barely keeping her voice steady. You bloody creep. "*Tror du att du får behandla mig som skit? Jag vet vad du har gjört.*" Do you think you can treat me like a piece of shit? I know what you've done.

"Jesus Chris, Ylva!" Dougie shouted at her, hanging his arms out like a scarecrow as he felt the beer soak into his sweater and run down the sleeves. Amber droplets spilling from his fingers.

"I know what you've done, you fucking bastard," she continued, switching to English to be sure he'd understand every word she had to say to him. So that he'd understand exactly how she felt and what she wanted him to do. "I know about the lies you've been telling. What you told him."

Dougie's face grew ashen as he realised what she was referring to. And Ylva saw from his expression that Karl hadn't been lying or embellishing anything. The entire pub was watching them. The fight in the arena; and let them watch. Let them see that not all Swedes avoided the problem and let people walk over them. Let them learn what a nasty, treacherous bastard Dougie really was. People glanced awkwardly at each other, or stared at the floor hoping they wouldn't get dragged into this. Someone sniggered to a friend that it was a lover's tiff.

"I could sue you for slander for what you've done."

"Look, Ylva..." he moved to stand up, perhaps take her roughly by the arm to drag her out of the pub, tell her off for creating a scene, scold her for embarrassing him. It wasn't just the Swedes who disliked making a public spectacle of themselves. Ylva instinctively kicked at the table. It jolted a little, enough to push him back into his chair.

"*Käften*! I think you've said more than enough. You keep away from me and my business. And if I ever heard that you've been spreading this shit about me again, I will destroy you, I swear to God."

"Ylva, this is a..."

"You don't speak to me. You don't speak about me. You don't see me and you don't come anywhere near me."

The landlord appeared, quite and disapproving. "Ylva, hen, I think we need to take this outside."

"I'm leaving now."

Dougie stood up. "I need to speak to you."

"Stay the fuck away from me." Ylva marched out of the pub with whatever little dignity she had left. She bit the side of her mouth, and although she could feel her eyes filling up, she did not cry, did not give that liar the satisfaction of seeing just how much he had destroyed her. She hurried back to her VW van and drove home to Broadford, the CD of folk music she'd bought playing loudly, the song about the insane murders on full volume to blot out her thoughts.

Over the next few days, Ylva gained a little appreciation of just how hard it could be to avoid someone. It was a taste of what it must have been like for Karl and his family going back to Sweden. But in comparison, they'd left like cowards, with no explanation. At least she'd had it out with Dougie and there was no ambiguity remaining. Everyone knew where they stood.

She stayed in her house that weekend and refused all calls. Texts from Morag went unanswered. Calls from Dougie were hung up. Emails sat unread in her email account. Lying in bed listening to the knocks on the door and not wanting to talk. She didn't care who it was. She was ashamed, she was a fool. She'd been taken for a ride. Whether it was Dougie, Morag, the landlady or even the postman, she did not wish to hear what they wanted to say to her. It felt as though everyone knew how stupid she had been. The trusting and naïve Swede. And the worst of it was, she didn't know why. Was it so foolish to move to another country and want to try to settle there? To make friends, create a life? Clearly it was, because Dougie had tried to destroy her business.

Ylva balled her fists up and stared out of the living room window. She clearly was a terrible judge of character. She would never have expected him to do something so underhand. Which just proved that she had no idea of who he really was. And was she so stupid even now? She couldn't work out why he had done it.

It was growing dark. A speck of light flickered in the far distance, as if someone had a little fire going on the beach. The outside world. She'd soon have to re enter it, because she had customers next week, and she could hardly hide in the house claiming a wounded soul. She had to get on with life. Show everyone that she was above it.

She leant back into the settee, her elbow catching uncomfortably on something. It was her knitting; her stress-releaving, relaxing activity. A blue scarf that was getting to a reasonable length. A scarf that had been promised to that treacherous, back-stabbing bastard. She threw it at the window. Maybe she should take the hint and leave Skye. It was a relatively big island with a good sized population, but it was still small enough to have to bump into the same people. She wasn't going to be able to do this.

Her mobile phone started ringing again. Ylva paused in her fury and picked the article up. The little screen displayed Morag's name. Ylva considered her options. It was now three days since she had caused a scene in the pub, and had not yet spoken to anyone. Morag had rung a surprising number of times, so she had to know about what had happened. She shouldn't really punish her friend – she hadn't done anything wrong.

"Hello?"

"Illvar? Thank god you're answering," Morag burst out. "Are you all right? I've not been able to get an answer out of you for days. Where've you been?"

"At home."

"Home?" Morag sounded surprised. "But you've not been answering the door."

"Doesn't mean I wasn't here" Jesus, she sounded like a stroppy brat. It wasn't as if Morag was involved. "I'm sorry; I've just not been one for company the last few days. I hope you didn't make a special trip down to Broadford."

"Oh, I didn't," Morag replied. "It's just what Dougie told me."

Ylva felt her upper lip curl.

"Ylva, hen, what's been going on?" Morag continued. "I hear there was a real drama down the pub. I've had Dougie over here twice; do you know that? He said he put a letter through the letterbox. Did you get it?"

She glanced in the direction of the front door. There was an envelope lying on the mat. "There's something over there. I don't intend on opening it. I'm not interested."

"But Illvar, you've got to let him…"

"I'm not interested."

"Have you checked the doorstep?"

"The doorstep?" Ylva raised her eyebrows. What was she talking about now? "I've not been out."

"Look, Dougie's told me what happened. He's told me everything. I really think you need to…"

"I don't want to hear his name," Ylva interrupted. "I'm not interested. I do not want to know. He does not exist."

"He does, hen…"

"No he does not."

"Illvar, you have to…"

"*Fy FAN!*" Ylva screeched down the phone. "I don't have to do a sodding thing. That lying bastard has been sabotaging my business. It's called slander. I want nothing more to do with him. You are not to mention his shitty name in my presence."

"Please, Illvar, you need to listen…" Morag persisted.

"NO. I'm not interested. Call me back when you have something else to say." She ended the call and switched off the phone. She didn't want to listen to a sob story about a cousin who was trying to get into business and needed to deal with the competition whilst battling a life-threatening disease and nursing ten battered kittens back to life; or how Dougie was just under a lot of pressure at work and said things he didn't mean – a coping mechanism, it was either that or crack cocaine; or maybe he was just concerned about local unemployment and felt strongly about the immigrant issue. She just did not want to hear the pathetic excuses. Because there was no good reason for what he had done.

Give it a few more days and Morag will accept that playing the peacemaker just isn't going to work, she said to herself as she drew her body up from the settee. This will all eventually blow over and people will move on. Dougie will learn to keep out of her way. And if it was too uncomfortable, then she'd just have to leave. She'd started a new life on Skye from scratch and she could do it again.

Exhausted, from the thinking, the silence, the nothing, the fury, the betrayal and the tears, for the first time in days she felt as though she could sleep. Time for bed. Wandering through to the bathroom, she switched on the light and stepped up to the sink. Squeezed out some toothpaste onto her toothbrush and started to clean her teeth. Looking down, she examined the plug hole. The whole sink looked grubby. She would have to conduct a serious clean of the house.

When she raised her head again to meet herself in the mirror, there was the reflection of a man standing in the doorway behind her. He had dark, tousled unruly hair; sun, wind-tanned skin; and a wry smile. Missing two teeth from the grin. His eyes sparkled, and there was something not quite right in the way that he looked at her.

Ylva almost choked back her toothbrush in horror. She spun around, ready to attack with whatever she could. She faltered, meeting no one in the doorway. She was alone. Fear pricked at her, and she felt it catch up in her eyes and her nose; tighten up her chest. Everything was ready to fall apart.

She looked back to the mirror, meeting her own terrified gaze. Beyond her he stood, still grinning. And now he was saying something, but she couldn't hear the words, because he was only a reflection in a mirror, and there was nothing solid behind her to make a sound. The toothbrush dropped to the floor. Ylva ducked into a defensive position, turning back to the bathroom doorway. He wasn't there.

"*Faaaaaan*," she wailed, running from the bathroom. As she ran through the house she turned on all the lights. Her eyes filling with tears. Grabbing her car keys from the side table, she struggled with the front door lock, suddenly desperate to get out of her home. Her sanctuary was no longer safe.

Stumbling outside, she tripped over something left on the doorstep, spilling flowers everywhere. It pulled her back, and she halted, looking at the mess in confusion. Picking up the destroyed bunch of flowers, she realised there was a note with them, immediately recognising Dougie's handwriting. "Fuck off, Dougie," she hissed at no one. Running down the rutted drive to the single-track road, she leaned over the seawall, throwing the flowers to the low lying rocks on the shore. She crumpled up the note in angry fingers, but couldn't quite bring herself to throw it away. She balled it up into her sweater pocket, and turned to walk back to her house, the wind creeping around her bare legs. Dressed in a mid-thigh skirt and hooded sweater, not warm enough for the evening chill.

The man was standing by her open front door when she returned. He was scruffily dressed, as if all of his clothes were too big for him. Stained trousers, misshapen shirt and a waistcoat like an afterthought. He smiled at her as she stopped, horrified that he had reappeared, that she had even forgotten about him for a moment in her anger at Dougie. Black holes gaped where teeth should have been.

"I've been waiting for you," he told her. "Now you and me's going to have some fun."

Ylva opened her mouth to do something, say something, scream, only if she could try and defend herself. He ran at her, catching her by the arms as she stumbled backwards, and nutted her neatly in the centre of her forehead. A nauseous burst came through before everything went black and the stranger disappeared from view.

She was cold. A chill was creeping down the length of her arms. She couldn't feel her legs. Ylva shivered. Cautiously she opened her eyes. Bewildered, staring up at the night sky; stars winking silently back down at her. Why was she here?

Slowly, stiffly, she sat up. She was on the grass outside her home, in the dark, with a bad headache and sore eyes. Raising her hands to brush tangled hair off her face, she realised she was clutching her car keys, the key rings and chains twisted around her fingers. Glancing over her shoulder, she saw that the front door was wide open; light blazing out from all of the windows. What was going on?

Her eyes drifted across to her legs, and she automatically gagged. Her bare legs stuck out from her mid-thigh blue skirt. Legs covered in blood. "*Vad fan...*" she whispered in an unstable voice, dabbing at her flesh and horrified to feel the wet, dissipating warmth of blood. Her fingers were sticky and thick with blood yet the cleaning effort had made no real impression on the carnage on her thighs.

"*Jävla.*" She scrambled up onto her feet, tripping backwards in the motion. She was outside, alone in the night with blood covering her thighs. Think, Ylva, think. Her hands were shaking as she closed her eyes, trying to remember. The front of her head stung.

She walked over to the van. Unlocking the driver's door, the light automatically came on. Ylva pulled down the sunshield and opened the mirror on the inner side. She stared at her white reflection, the start of a bruise in the middle of her forehead. Looking in a mirror. And he had been staring back at her.

She slammed the sun shield back up in a panic. That crazy guy must have attacked her, torn at her legs. She could remember him lunging, as if going for her head, then nothing. And she had seen his reflection in the bathroom mirror, but when she had turned around he had not been there. He must have ducked out of the way. But she couldn't see him anywhere now. Her eyes drifted across to the open front door. What if he was waiting in the house for her?

Ylva pulled the driver's door to; pushing down the internal lock. Her fingers were shaking again. She felt giddy. What was it you were supposed to do when you were attacked? She felt a sob catch in the back of her throat. She looked back down at her legs, at the blood. Leaning across the front of the van, she pulled open the glove box for her first aid kit. It didn't open easily, and she had to tug at the handle. Then everything came spilling out suddenly, falling into the foot well, and she couldn't see anything for the driver door light had switched off as she'd shut the door. In the dark she heard herself whimper. Her hands moved through the near-empty glove box, and found her emergency mobile phone – a cheap pay-as-you-go mobile she left permanently in the van for emergencies. She switched the phone on. This counted as an emergency.

When the police car pulled up outside her house, Ylva had calmed down a little, although she was still locked inside the van, keys resting in the ignition ready to speed away – as if she had enough strength and control in her legs to drive. Two police officers stepped out of the vehicle: one, Hamish Jones, she knew vaguely, and the woman she didn't recognise at all. Perhaps she was the new recruit Hamish had said they were getting.

Whilst waiting, she had found a box of tissues and wiped off a lot of the blood. At one point she had hoped that for some reason it wasn't her blood. It was. Wiping away at the covering revealed the incisions into her thighs – roughly round circles, about five or six centimetres in diameter. No skin had been removed, no flesh dug out, only a polka dot pattern of red-lined, weeping outline circles in her legs. It looked as though a roaming psychopath had started to carve her up.

Ylva opened the driver door, waving to the police officers. Other sane human beings – thank god, she thought. She stepped from the van and felt her legs wobble. She was like a rag doll, drained of energy.

"Ullba Johansson," Hamish greeted her. "We had a call put through that you'd been attacked?" He sounded as though he didn't believe it. Skye was not a perfect, law abiding state – there was the odd bit of vandalism, theft, drug abuse and alcohol-fuelled issues, but roaming random psychotic attacks were not regular occurrences.

"I don't know if he's in the house or run off," Ylva said, surprised by how monotone she sounded. Surely she ought to be hysterical. "I've just locked myself in the van."

"You didn't want to drive away?"

Holding on to the side of the van, she took a couple of steps forward. "I feel like I've had the stuffing kicked out of me."

Both officers saw her legs, lit up from the light blaring out of her cottage. "Jesus," Hamish muttered. "Annabel, will you go and call the police surgeon from the car. Get them to meet us back at the station."

The woman hurried to the police car. Hamish led Ylva around to rest on the driver's seat. "We'll be away back to the station; get you checked over, take a statement, if you can manage it tonight," he paused, looking down at Ylva's legs, the bottom of her thighs showing from under the skirt. "Jesus, lass, what's been going on?"

"I don't know," she answered, feeling her voice start to crack. "I was just getting ready for bed and then there was this man in my house. I ran outside and he went for me. Knocked me out. When I woke up I was lying on the grass outside. And my legs…" she held out her hands, looking back down at her legs. She didn't know how to explain any of this.

"Do these cuts go all the way up?"

"Most of the way. They stop about here." She placed a hand in her lap at the top of her legs. She looked miserably down at her chilly flesh. Why would anyone want to do something like this to someone else?

"Like mince pies in thighs," Hamish muttered quietly to himself.

Ylva looked up sharply at him. "What did you say?"

"Oh, nothing, ignore me."

There was something familiar about those words. Ylva squinted at him. "Song lyrics."

He looked surprised by what she had said, but they didn't have chance to continue their conversation as Annabel returned. "He's on his way," she said.

"Right, you stay here with Ylva. I'll check this nutter's not still about. It looks as though he's scarpered. Can I take your house keys, Ylva? I'll lock up once I've checked."

"They're still inside. On the hall table."

Hamish set off to check the area. "Shall we go back to the car?" Annabel asked, "We'll drive you over to the station and get you sorted."

"Sure." Ylva stood up and shut the door. She went to lock the door, but her hands were shaking again and she dropped the keys in the dirt.

"Let me get that." Annabel crouched and picked up the keys. She locked the van, then escorted Ylva over to the police car. Ylva was helped into the back seat without a word. Annabel went around to open the boot and came back with a tartan blanket. "Keep yourself warm," she advised.

Sitting down in the passenger seat, she twisted around to watch Ylva. "Do you feel like you can tell me what happened?"

"There's not a lot to tell," Ylva said, staring steadily out of the front windscreen. She pulled the blanket around her body. "I was brushing my teeth and I saw him in the mirror. This man. I ran out of the house. I remember him coming at me, like he was going to nut me…"

"You have got a wee bruise on your forehead," Annabel pointed out.

"I must have blacked out. I woke up freezing, and with this on my legs. I wiped off a lot of the blood whilst I was waiting for you."

"So you don't remember him cutting your legs?"

She shook her head.

"Things may come back to you in the next few days," Annabel told her. "You may even get the feeling that something might have happened." She paused awkwardly. She hadn't been in the force particularly long and didn't have much special training for this kind of thing. But they were short staffed, it was two in the morning and Hamish had presumed that because she was female, she'd be good at it. He had been adamant in the car on their way here that he wasn't going to have 'the talk'. "Do you think he might have...?"

Ylva's eyes flickered to Annabel's uncomfortable face.

"Well, what I mean is, do you think there's any chance that you were raped?"

"Sorry?"

"Well, we have to consider it. You were unconscious, and there was a man in your house..." Annabel faltered again.

"I don't know. I don't think so." Ylva felt sick. Her legs involuntarily squeezed in close together, as if that would help her now. She didn't feel any pain down between her legs. Surely if she'd been raped she would have felt it, would have instinctively known? Was that the way it went? She had been knocked unconscious; he could have done anything to her. They said women who were date raped with rohypnol felt there was something wrong, even though they couldn't remember the actual event.

"Don't worry about it now," Annabel quickly told her. "The police surgeon will deal with all of that. Tell me about the man instead. Do you know him?"

Ylva shook her head.

"So you've not seen him before?"

"No. I've no idea who he is. I've never seen him before." She looked down into the shadows where her feet were placed. Her brow crinkled in thought. "Although maybe..."

"Maybe?"

"Maybe I did see him once before." She was thinking of his grin, the smile with two black holes were teeth should have been. She'd seen that before, briefly but this wasn't the first time.

"Where was that?"

"Glen Brittle," Ylva said. "Glen Brittle beach; quite a few weeks ago. I went to a beach party."

"And he was at the beach party?" Annabel sounded urgent.

"No." Ylva was sure on that point. She hadn't seen him before or during that beach party. Just standing out in the sea near her. And when Dougie had come over, the man had disappeared, sneaking off into the night. That was the only other occasion she had seen him, but after all that time for him to now appear and attack her was very random. Perhaps he had been watching her the last few weeks. Maybe this was more planned than the course of events might suggest. "It was just a fleeting moment, him passing by." She looked back up at Annabel. "Do you think I have a stalker?"

"I'm not sure. It's possible, but…" she couldn't think of anything reassuring to say just now. "We'll get this sorted. Don't worry."

"There's no one about." Hamish said as he opened the driver's door. "I've checked the house and locked it up. It's quite empty. Are you all right to head back to the station?"

Ylva nodded meekly. There was nowhere else to go.

Ylva almost turned and fled from the building when Annabel led her to a small side office where the police surgeon was waiting. She did not want to go in. Judging from the expression on the police surgeon's face, he was ready to leave as well. She had just experienced the worst episode in her life, and now to finish the whole awfulness of it, she had to go through some kind of examination ordeal.

Of course, she should have made the connection when Hamish mentioned the police surgeon. The police employed medical examiners who were specially for the deceased of course, but in the case of the wounded and battered, they often had a regular G.P. on their books who would be called out when required. There were a couple on Skye, and she knew from past conversations that Dougie was one of them.

Being a relative stranger, Annabel obviously hadn't heard about the drama at the pub, and even if she had, she wouldn't have realised that she was now bringing the two protagonists into the same room. And she just kept leading Ylva in towards the high bench made up as an examination table. Ylva felt as though she had to play along, as if not to hurt the poor girl's feelings. It was three in the morning. Who else were they going to get?

"Dr MacWhirter," Annabel greeted Dougie, "This is Ullba Johansson. She was attacked some time after midnight. She was unconscious for a period; we think she was hit on the forehead. There's some cuts on her legs."

That much ought to have been apparent from the neat round bruise on her head and her bloodied legs. Ylva felt sick as she walked across the room and hopped onto the examination table. Sitting up straight, she let her legs hang over the edge.

"I'll have to get some photographic evidence," Annabel added, still the only person to speak. Ylva watched her in bewildered awe as the girl carefully photographed her face and her legs. Could she not feel the tension, notice that everyone else here was acutely uncomfortable? This one wasn't going to make a detective.

Annabel placed the camera at the side of the room. "Right, I think that's all we need…"

Ylva looked desperately across at her. "You're not going are you?"

"Well, you don't need me here."

"Please!"

Annabel misread the terror on Ylva's face. Thinking she needed female support, that she was skittish around strange men after what had happened, she smiled in a kindly way. She sat down in a chair. "Don't worry; I'll stay in the room with you."

Dougie looked tired. It was more than a late night call out that had probably disturbed sleep, but perhaps more that he wasn't sleeping well in general. Overall exhaustion. He looked wary of Ylva, as if she might turn and lash out at him. Frustrated that the young P.C. was staying. They would have to keep up this charade of strained polite conversation.

He put his bag beside Ylva's seated frame and stepped up to her, perhaps a little closer than was strictly necessary. He looked down at her legs. He looked miserable. "Jesus, Ylva," he said quietly. "Who did this to you?"

"Unidentified male," Annabel answered for her, and Ylva silently thanked her for dealing with the question.

Ylva hiked up her skirts so that all of the circles were visible. She dared a glance across at Dougie, who was looking as though this pained him more than it pained her.

He had a cotton swab with antiseptic and started to clean up her wounds. Ylva audibly winced as she felt the antiseptic bite. Most of the cut lines appeared to have congealed; only a couple were still weeping; the scabs probably breaking open with movement as she'd hopped up onto the bench.

"What do you think was used to make the cuts?" Annabel asked.

"A knife," Dougie said simply. "A small sharp knife. Or a piece of broken glass."

He ran the cotton around one of the circles on her thigh. Ylva could feel the latex-enclosed fingers brush by her skin. This was excruciatingly uncomfortable. She had an overwhelming desire to slap him, but had to behave for Annabel. This had to be the worst day of her life.

"They don't appear to be too deep. Cuts seem to be clean. They should heal up on their own." He continued up her legs. "This one will need a stitch," he added, gently touching a particularly deep cut high up on her right thigh. This one looked as though the attacker had sliced deep enough to try and scoop out the flesh. "Do you want anything for the pain?"

"Just get it done," Ylva said tersely. Her eyes were closed as she felt the needle go into her skin. Hands gripped the edge of the bed. She could feel her eyes welling up, not just because her thigh was being stitched, but because of what had happened, what might have happened; the way everything had worked out. A week ago her life had been reasonably settled. Contented. Now she was in this hellish place.

"We'll just keep some simple bandaging around these," Dougie spoke, his voice quite weak and forced as he worked before the audience of Annabel. "To keep it clean. You might get a little bit of bleeding; just lines of blood as scabs crack open with movement. It's nothing to worry about. But keep it clean so it doesn't get infected. We'll get one of the district nurses to come over to change the dressing for you."

Ylva keep her eyes closed as she felt the bandages being wrapped around her legs. She wanted to step right out of this situation, out of this life, this country, this skin. She heard Dougie pull the gloves off.

"I'll just check where Hamish has got to," Annabel said.

She heard the chair squeak as Annabel got up. Something gagged and caught in her throat. Dougie's manner changed as soon as the girl was out of the room. "Jesus, Ylva. What the hell's happened to you?"

She couldn't talk to him. She managed to open her eyes, but her anger was back, and she couldn't look him in the eye.

Dougie leaned in closer, his head almost touching hers. "Look, Ylva, please," he whispered, his voice strained. "I'm so sorry about what happened. I panicked…"

"Stop talking." She felt sick. He was sorry, but he wouldn't deny what had been done. There was no handy back door to take out of this unpleasantness. He really had told those lies about her. Stabbed her in the back.

"Just taking a cigarette," Annabel reappeared in the room.

Dougie had abruptly stepped away from Ylva again. Back in the charade for Annabel's sake. "We're done here."

Annabel raised her eyebrows, not looking convinced. So desperate to get this right. "But don't you need to take some swabs or something?"

"Swabs?"

"Miss Johansson was unconscious for a period. We don't know what kind of attack this was."

She was met with silence.

Annabel looked frustrated. She didn't want to have to spell it out. "Well, don't you need to examine her? She might have been interfered with…"

"No!" Ylva's voice was surprisingly loud, exaggerated by the intense quietness of the hours after midnight. Today had been bad enough as it was, and she had endured up to the limit of what she was capable of coping with. There was no chance she was enduring any kind of gynaecological examination performed by Dougie. "I'm leaving. Right now."

Annabel looked pained; terrified she'd said something wrong. "We only need to make sure."

Dougie threw Annabel an angry glance. "Ylva, I'm not doing anything you don't want…"

"I'm leaving." Ylva swept out of the room, running blindly down the corridor. Pushing against the door, she staggered out into the night and the chilly air. There were tears in her eyes. She wiped at her eyes with the back of her hand, glancing around the virtually empty car park, not sure where to go.

"All done, Ullba?" The glowing light from the end of Hamish's cigarette proceeded him as he walked over.

She turned around. Hamish; thank god. "Yes," she told him. "I'd like to go now."

"Sure, I'll drive you," he said calmly. He knew as well as she did that they hadn't taken a statement yet, but judging from her expression and her body language, she'd had enough for one day. She needed to sleep. "Do you have someone who can come and stay with you? I don't suppose you'll want to be on your own."

Who could she call on? In other circumstances, she would have said Dougie without thinking, but her friend had proven himself to be her enemy. And Morag had been so pleading on that she didn't want to hear more violins on Dougie's behalf. Plus she wouldn't want to scare Morag's children with her mutilated legs. "Could you give me a lift to Colm's house?" she finally decided. "He'll let me stay over there tonight."

"Sure," Hamish nodded, opening the passenger door. "Hop in and I'll drive you over there. You can give him a ring on the way in you like, make sure he's about."

"He keeps funny hours," Ylva said as she got into the car. "He won't mind."

The car pulled out of the car park and on to the main road. Ylva was relieved when they had started the journey, thankful that neither Annabel nor Dougie had followed her outside. Hamish flicked on the headlights. "So old Doc Anderson was all right to you?" he asked. "Not too grumpy we'd dragged him out of bed?"

"It wasn't Anderson."

"Oh no?" Hamish raised his eyebrows, his brain ticking it over logically. If it hadn't been so late at night, he may have anticipated this in advance, stopped Annabel from doing something stupid. He glanced over at Ylva, now worried. "She didn't call in Dougie, did she?"

"Yes."

"Shit," Hamish cursed. "I thought you two had a falling out the other day. You not made up yet?"

"Not the kind of thing you can come back from."

Hamish raised his eyebrows and knew better than to ask for details.

After a period of silence, Ylva found her voice again. "Hamish, when you first came to collect me, you said that thing about mince pies. You remember?

Hamish pursed his lips and looked distinctly uncomfortably. "I didn't find anyone when I checked your house and looked around the area. You know, there wasn't any sign of a break in," he stopped. "Look, I've got to be professional, I can't suggest…."

Ylva looked horrified. "You think this was all in my head?"

"Oh lord no," Hamish shook his head. "Someone cut your legs. That I have no doubt about."

There was something he was holding back. "Do you think you know who?"

"I can't say anything."

"You're the police!"

"It's not like that."

"Well, what is it like?"

He was considering it. Wondering if he would come to regret this conversation. Because, really, it was very unprofessional. "Maybe you should go and tell my old man about this sometime. You know where the farm is?"

"Well, yes, but what would your father…?"

"I can't say anymore." He shook his head. "Not doing the job I do."

The thing with friends, close friends, was that you always presumed that they had your best interests at heart. That they cared about your life as much as you did. That there could never be any conflict. But deep down, everyone is selfish, everyone is alone in their battles and you can't truly rely on anyone.

Ylva lay in bed and stared at the ceiling. When she had gone to the pub to confront Dougie, there had been part of her hoping that he would deny it. Because to spread such malicious lies was so out of character for Dougie. At least how she had defined his character to herself. They would eventually laugh about how stupid Karl had been for making things up. But there was no logical reason for Karl to lie, at least not that Ylva could think of. Just as she didn't really understand why Dougie had done it. But he was guilty. He had never attempted to deny the accusations; in fact the guilt on his face was clear. He knew that she had been told and he was 'sorry' for what he had done. It didn't make it any better. It didn't mean that she could trust him again.

When the police car had pulled up outside Colm's house in the wee small hours of the morning, Colm had been sitting on the doorstep smoking a cigarette. He looked unfazed by the proceedings, shrugging in a nonchalant way as if it were to be expected.

Ylva had taken Colm's bed; Colm saying he would doze on the sofa – probably already had taken his night's quota of sleep, anyway. She hadn't thought she would be able to sleep, but she lost consciousness very quickly. Emotionally and physically exhausted by what had happened, her body was happy to switch off from the world for a while, only regretful that she would have to wake up again.

She didn't manage to sleep for long. Her eyes opened and she was wide awake. The bare minimum of hours and now her body wanted to get going. She looked at her watch. Half past six in the morning.

Rolling out of bed, she walked across the landing to the bathroom. Standing in front of the mirror, she examined her sallow tinted face. There were voices outside, a little faded as if they were around the front of the house. Colm was already up – he hadn't been joking when he said he wouldn't have much sleep coming.

"...should have gone away as planned...some nutter roaming about..." She heard Colm's voice. Visitors already? Perhaps Hamish was back to get a statement from her, although this was very early for routine business. He had told her last night in the car to just come back to the station sometime today when she felt ready for it. Ylva stepped up to the bathroom window, open a chink and strained to catch the words.

"So you two had a falling out or something?" Colm asked.

Ylva's eyes widened.

"...misunderstanding..." Dougie's voice wafted up around the house.

She pressed her back against the wall, not wanting to leave an image in the frosted glass for all to see. Damn it, Dougie was here? She glanced at her watch again. Why was he at Colm's house at half six in the morning? Colm's place was up a little track, so you couldn't even use the excuse of just passing.

"Aye," Dougie continued. A few sentences she couldn't catch. "...no, I screwed it up to be honest...."

Ylva looked down at her legs. Her skirt didn't cover the bottom of the bandages; like scruffy, inelegant leg warmers on the wrong part of her body. She still couldn't quite comprehend what had happened last night. Drawing up her skirt, she examined the full length of her bandages. There were a couple of lines of blood where the scabs must have cracked open in her sleep. She wondered if she'd have permanent scarring from this; if she'd be restricted to trousers for the rest of her life. Rather than to show the world the mince pies on her legs. What did that mean anyway? Hamish had said something about it yesterday. Said his father would know.

A car engine started up. Catching her breath, she dared to twist across and peer through the corner of the window. A vehicle left Colm's house, back down the single track to the main road. Dougie was gone.

Downstairs in the kitchen, Colm was putting the kettle on. He glanced up as Ylva padded bare foot into the room. "*Morgon*, kiddo," he said, mixing his languages. "Your mate's just been over."

"Dougie?"

Colm raised his eyebrows. "Listening at the window? Aye, it was Dougie. I told him you weren't here. I get the impression you two aren't on speaking terms at the moment."

Ylva slumped at the kitchen table. "That's very astute of you," she commented. "Although I suspect the whole island's gossiping about it."

Colm laughed as he prepared tea in a couple of chipped mugs. "Don't think of yourself too highly on the island. You're not the height of gossip round here, you know. Anyway, I hear you're away back to Sweden soon?"

"What?"

"Back to the homeland for a new job?"

"No."

"Oh." He pursed his lips for a moment, and shrugged, as if to say that he didn't really care either way. "Must have heard it wrong." He sat down opposite her and pushed a mug of milky tea in her direction. "You garbled on the phone last night."

"Sorry?"

"When you rang. I didn't catch much at all, even when you landed. You going to tell me what's been going on?"

"Oh," she said, realising what he meant. She looked down at her tea, the steam twisting off the surface and into the kitchen atmosphere. The light was cool, clear and sharp. The air silent. No space for ambiguity. "It almost doesn't feel like it happened now; this morning, in daylight."

"That'll be the shock for you," Colm advised as he slurped his tea. "The adrenaline keeping you going. Give it a few days and you'll fall to pieces."

Ylva looked up at him sourly. "I'm not some fragile little princess."

"All right then, you robust, big wench…"

"Sod off, Colm."

He laughed. "What's been going on?"

"I was attacked last night. At home. This guy was in my house. I ran out and he followed me and knocked me out. When I woke up, my legs were hacked up."

"That'll explain the trendy shorts." Colm leant back in his chair. "So this wasn't someone you knew? Just a headcase passing by? Jesus," he shook his head to himself. "I would have thought Skye would be a safe place for a woman to live on her own. Well, aye, there's problems: the isolation and the natural elements; but you cope with all that just fine. Still, there's no accounting for nutters. They can pop up anywhere."

He made it sound like a slight accident; a short blip from the peace and quiet. No need to worry; it wasn't like the lunatic was going to come back.

"We seem to be having a spate of it; what with all the cat bonfires." Colm looked disgusted.

Burning cats. Nutcases and mince pies. She felt as though she was missing something obvious. She scratched her leg just above the bottom rim of her bandages. It was uncomfortable to have this much padding permanently wound around her thighs. "I'm going to have to go home and get changed. I look stupid like this. I need some jeans on. Can you give me a lift?"

"Sure," Colm nodded.

"I'll have to drive up to the police station and leave a statement." Ylva drummed her fingers on the kitchen table. "Shit," she suddenly burst out.

"What's up now?"

"Oh no." She lowered her head to the kitchen table. "I just remembered, I have a group of day trippers today. "*Fan, fan, fan.* What am I going to do with them?"

"What did you have planned?"

"Loch Coruisk. We were getting the boat from Elgol up there."

Colm considered it over for a moment. "I'll take them round if you like. Just this once, mind."

"Really?"

"You're paying me, you understand."

"Yes, of course." That was one less thing to think about. She doubted she could have played happy host, showing yet more paying guests around the island, hiking around the interior lock of the Cullins on her battered legs. Grinning and enthusing about the dramatic scenery. Trying to blot out the lunatic's broken grin.

Colm turned his mug around on the table. "We've got to be adaptable. Things change." He paused. "I hear Morag's got a new fella."

Ylva looked up sharply. Morag. This must be the first time Colm had ever mentioned her friend to her. Morag had told her that she and Colm had enjoyed a brief fling last summer, but Ylva had never completely believed her. "Yes, she's told me that. Won't tell me who."

"I know who."

"Who is it?" Ylva leaned forward. Colm merely eyed her. "It's not you?"

He laughed. "Jesus no. Someone a bit younger." He didn't make any offer to educate her further. "Although you maybe already know; you lassies talk about all sorts. We had a bit of something last year. Would have been nice to pick it up again." He stood up, gazed nostalgically out of the kitchen window, then turned his back on Ylva to swill out his tea mug. It was quite clear that the subject for discussion was now closed.

Ylva stared at his back. That was as close as she would ever see Colm admit to regrets. It was so sad: if only he had enough sense or guts to say something. There was no rewind button on time, and he had missed his chance. She felt something catch in the back of her throat. It really did happen at times; not everyone got their happy ending; people that might have been together, ended up separate and moving onwards with their lives. Sometimes it was just life, but when you saw that it had been in their power, it was heart-breaking.

"I'll give you a lift back to Broadford," Colm interrupted her philosophising. "Then you can get yourself back up to the police station; leave your statement in."

Mr Jones, father of Hamish Jones of the Skye constabulary, opened the front door of his old farmhouse as the vehicle drove up the track. He was awaiting a hip operation, and didn't walk particularly well, needing the aid of a stick to carry him. His grey hair, fine like sand, blew in the wind. He watched the converted camper van park up beside his own battered car. A young blonde woman got out of the driver's seat – the Swede living on the island the last couple of years.

"Mr Jones?"

"Aye," he nodded to her.

Ylva approached, not sure how to start this conversation. She was here because Hamish had hinted that his father knew something, but would say no more. It had been quite vague – as if he might know who had attacked her, but didn't want to say. Surely it was his duty, given his profession. Perhaps he was evasive because it was someone known to the family? Or he was guessing, and knew what unfounded suggestions could do to people's reputations and lives. She honestly wasn't sure what to expect. The only concrete sensation at the moment was that she didn't feel comfortable going back home. It would be a start to know who that man had been; where he was now. A promise he wouldn't be back.

"My name's Ylva Johansson," she introduced herself.

"Aye." He nodded a second a time. "You'll be that Swedish lassie working on the island."

The wind rattled up the hillside at a fair pace, blowing her hair across her face. Ylva pushed it out of her eyes, wondering if this conversation would go anywhere. "I've come because your son, Hamish suggested it."

"Oh aye?"

"Has Hamish mentioned me at all?" she asked hopefully. She didn't want to go into lengthy explanations again. She had just finished her statement at the police station. That was enough. Having to relive the attack, explain herself, justify the facts. It was as if she was the one to be punished for being attacked.

"He did," Mr Jones confirmed. "You were attacked in your home last night. It's a sad day indeed when good people aren't safe in their homes."

Oh Jesus, Ylva thought, Hamish has sent me on a wild goose chase. "Hamish thought you might know who attacked me."

"Did he now?" Mr Jones raised his wiry and particularly long eyebrows. "You and your friend there had best be coming in out of the wind."

She had come here alone. Ylva looked concerned. "What friend?"

"The lass by the gate there. She's with you."

Ylva twisted to look back down the track but she couldn't see anyone. "I don't see her. I'm not looking in the right place. Not that it matters, I came here on my own."

He watched; a little smile on his lips as Ylva was scanning the hillside. "You are looking in the wrong place. I was meaning right here; the gate beside your van."

Ylva dropped her eyes. "There's no one there."

"You don't see her?"

There was no one to see. Was the old man a bit nutty?

"A young lass with curly chestnut hair. She's got her boots in her hands." He paused, watching Ylva's expression. From blank to concern, a memory triggered. "But you think you've seen her before? I think I'm beginning to see why Hamish sent you."

"I have bumped into a woman of that description a couple of times, but she's not here now." Ylva scrabbled through her bag, pulling out the dog-eared print out Callum had given her. "This is the woman I've seen."

Mr Jones took his glasses out of his shirt pocket, looking at the wind-flicked paper. "That's her. And that's you there." He paused for breath as the wind snatched it from his mouth. "Strange choice of attire for the beach."

"It was an advertising campaign," Ylva mumbled.

"Where else have you seen her?"

"Portree. Uig; well, just outside of Uig. On the road down from Portree." She halted. "You're serious when you say you see her?"

"She's stood by your van. By, she's latched on to you."

"But..." Ylva took the photograph back, returning her eyes to her van. There was definitely no one there.

"Come on inside," Mr Jones offered, retreating in through his front door. "I'm sure Maud'll be fine outside. She'll be used to the wind."

The volume on the wind dropped as the front door was closed. Ylva followed the old man through to the kitchen. It was a proper crofter's cottage inside. It had a few nods to modern living, with the electric light in the ceiling and the white goods at the back end of the kitchen. The original fireplace and range were still in place, perhaps more for decoration than use these days. A heavy wooden table, decades of knife cuts from food preparation, feint washed away stains from meals and spilled drink.

"I'll make a pot of tea."

Ylva set her satchel of papers cautiously on the edge of the table. "I'm not sure I understand. This woman you say you see..."

"Maud?"

"Well, yes," she started, as though she were humouring him. "There's no one out there. So either you're seeing things or..."

"Or she's a ghost," Mr Jones finished for her. "Aye, I didn't say Maud was living. But she's there and she's latched on to you."

Ylva wasn't a believer, but neither was she an adamant non-believer when it came to the supernatural. It wasn't really something that came up, or that gave her reason to ponder the possibilities. She enjoyed reading local ghost stories, books on folklore and superstition, but she took it all in on a fiction level. It didn't register as something she might go tripping upon during her travels around the island. But Mr Jones had neatly described this haunting woman who had recently been appearing. Ylva wasn't sure she knew what the stranger was, but was unsure whether she was ready to accept the existence of ghosts. Because if Maud was a ghost, and she had latched onto Ylva, what did that mean for Ylva's chances of survival? Didn't ghosts mean bad news on the long-life front?

"She's perfectly harmless," Mr Jones commented as he put the kettle on and prepared the teapot. "If that's what's worrying you. She was harmless in life; harmless in death."

"Well, at least that's something," Ylva said. "I'd actually come to speak to you about something far more solid and real. A man attacked me last night…"

"But Maud doesn't come on her own," Mr Jones continued as if he hadn't heard a word. "And if I've understood what my son told me correctly, you've been visited by Tom."

"Tom?" Two mugs were set unceremoniously on the table in front of her. She felt her stomach pull back slightly, not because of the tea, but for the name. Connecting that lunatic up to a person. Mr Jones did know who had attacked her. "He was the man who attacked me?"

"I believe so." The old man poured the boiling water into the teapot. "Hamish said your legs had been cut; you've had small circles carved into your flesh."

"Hamish said mince pies."

Mr Jones raised his eyebrows as he set the teapot on the table.

"There's a folksong I like. It has a verse about this. Cutting mince pies out of children's thighs…"

"With which to feed the fairies," Mr Jones finished for her as he sat down. "I know that song well. Bedlam Boys."

"But that is just an old folk song." Ylva paused. She'd like to say Mr Jones was just a fanciful old man with a weakened grasp on reality. But his eyes were sharp, his memory keen. "If you're suggesting that this woman is a ghost…" she faltered. It sounded so stupid saying the word out loud, but she was actually starting to feel nervous with the suggestion. "Then what does that make him?"

"Tom's a special case," Mr Jones started. "But he's dead as far as you and I are concerned."

"You're suggesting a ghost did this to me? Have you seen the state of my legs?" she sounded angry.

"He's not exactly a ghost in the same sense as Maud. He's a man stuck in limbo." He stopped and poured out the tea. "But they come as a pair. I can't think why they've latched on to you, but they have. You don't look as though you believe me."

"I don't really know what to think."

"This all happened a long time ago, you understand," Mr Jones started to explain. "A couple of hundred years ago. Maud was born to a poor crofter's family up in Uig. Life was tough then. Not as tough though, as for the family Tom came from. They really were poor. Never a penny to their name and scrimping off the charity of the parish. The children went barefoot.

"The first time Maud and Tom met, Maud was a young girl. She was bringing a basket back to the home, and on crossing a wee burn, she tripped and fell into the water. The child would have surely drowned, if Tom hadn't gone in after and rescued her. He was her knight in armour, and she only ever had eyes for Tom after that. Lord knows why because he wasn't the most attractive of men, and he had a nasty streak in him. He was quite mad as well.

"Well, Tom left the island and broke Maud's heart…"

"She died of a broken heart?"

"Ach, no, that came later. No one knows exactly how far south Tom got, although he said he reached London. Rumour was he spent some time in Bedlam. People weren't sure how he could afford it, going south, I mean; for Tom's family was poverty stricken, yet the lad left well-clothed and shod. There were rumours, but he left the island and people thought no more of it. Then a few years later, he was back, worse for wear and missing a few teeth, but quite well off, and settled in Broadford for the few months before his disappearance."

"Broadford?" That was where Ylva lived.

"Then people agreed it must be true, Tom had found the cave in the Cullins." He stopped to take a drink of tea. "They say somewhere in the Cullins there is a cave of gold. It's not known where it is, but if you find it, there is enough wealth for your fortune ten times over. There's no beast to fight to get in, and once you know your way, you can return as many times as you like to refill your pockets."

"But this is just folklore."

"And there's a lot of truth in it. The catch with the cave is that every time you go in, every time you spend that gold, you grow a little more evil; loose a little more of your soul. And that is what happened to Tom. He was quite mad and it only got worse. All the locals knew he was practising the rite of Taghairm, for he wanted to make a deal with the devil."

"Taghairm," Ylva almost whispered the word. "Roasting cats alive to make contact with the devil. You know someone's been doing that recently on Broadford bay?"

"I've read it in the papers. Although they made no mention of Taghairm. They only said animal cruelty. I don't suppose they want to go putting ideas into people's heads. It's not a wise thing to do, because it never fares well. They say Tom brought out the devil, and wanted to be taken into hell."

"Well, surely he would have taken someone like that."

"Ah, but the devil couldn't take him. For Tom had performed one selfless act and saved the life of another, so he could not be taken into hell. But likewise he had done countless wicked things, so heaven wouldn't take him. He was condemned to walk the earth in limbo."

"What about Maud? She wasn't wicked, was she?"

"Stupid, perhaps," Mr Jones conceded, "Obsessed with a man who neither could nor would return her love. But wicked, no. She disappeared about the same time Tom disappeared, and no one ever found out what happened to her. Although people say he took her life in desperation to get accepted into hell. You see, as soon as Maud heard news that Tom was back on Skye, she took herself away from Uig and walked all the way south to Broadford. People saw her, said they saw her carrying her shoes over her shoulder, so that she wouldn't wear out the soles. It's said she got almost as far as Broadford, but then she disappeared. Probably met Tom; and the pair of them were never seen again."

Ylva ran a finger around the edge of her cup. "Well, it's an interesting story."

"It's no story; it's true. These people were alive upon this land once. And now they walk it for eternity." He leaned forward, peering closely at Ylva. "And for some reason, they've latched on to you. What they would want with a girl from Sweden, I do not know. But they must be after something; either that or they've nothing better to do."

She felt mildly irritated. What would they want with an outsider – he'd as good as said it. "You're not expecting me to go back to the police and say I was attacked by a ghost, are you?"

"I'm not expecting you to do anything," Mr Jones chuckled. "You came here to ask my opinion, and I've given you it. What you decide to do with the information is your own business."

Ylva looked grimly down at her cup. "I don't believe in ghosts," she muttered, almost sounding as though she were trying to convince herself of the fact.

"That may well be," Mr Jones said. "But by the sounds of things, they very much believe in you."

The wind was restless. Howling relentlessly. Skye was cast in grey. In the square in Portree, a bus had just departed, and there were few people loitering in the elements. Certainly no one was waiting; people were quick to continue on their journeys. On the lampposts the great flags of the Scottish tourist board flapped and rippled against the air currents. Images printed on cloth, colours suggesting eyes, staring out like sirens. In an image of Broadford bay stood Ylva; the dress she was wearing blown as much as the picture she was now trapped in. A distance of sand. She was unreachable.

At the bottom of the pole stood a forlorn figure, shrinking back into his jacket, his attention consumed by the movement of that particular flag. Dr Douglas MacWhirter. Ylva stumbled to an awkward halt at the street corner when she saw him. She didn't want a confrontation of any description. It was stupid to be in Portree when she was so keen to avoid him. But she had stopped off for a few things on the way back from Mr Jones' homestead. Certain that coincidence and misfortune could not be that unkind and put him in her path. At least Dougie had his back to the road she was on, and she ought to be able to sneak back unnoticed the way she had come.

But she lingered for a moment, too busy with voyeurism to go home. It was a forlorn, quite tragic scene, and it actually made her feel worse than she already did, although for something that wasn't quite as obvious as a man in the cold suffering from guilt of mistakes performed in haste.

Morag appeared at the far side of the square and waved. "Hey, you!"

Ylva jumped, shrinking back towards the building wall, horrified that Dougie would turn and see her watching. But Morag hadn't seen her. Dougie looked up as Morag approached. Said something Ylva couldn't hear. Morag tilted her head to consider the doctor, replying in a low voice. Then they were up close and Morag was wrapping her arms around him. It was reciprocated.

The wind blew and Ylva was suddenly gagging for breath. She hurried back down the road, shocked to find her legs were shaking. It felt as though a giant was squeezing her torso between two meaty hands. She could barely remember where she had left the van. Erratic footsteps clattering down the stone steps to the car park by the seafront. And Ylva was scrambling for her keys, her fingers taking their own dance and she dropped the bunch of keys. "*Fy...*" she cursed hollowly at herself, ducking down to retrieve the keys; the wind blowing her hair across her vision. She wretched the door open and threw herself into the van.

With a thump of the door the wind became background noise and the air was still. Ylva felt giddy. She pulled down the sun shield, looking at herself in the little mirror. She was shocked to see her eyes watering, the salty tears pouring down her face. It was the wind; so vicious. Either that or delayed shock. Colm had said it would hit her at some point. The delayed shock from last night's attack.

Dunking her forehead on to the steering wheel, Ylva groaned: "*Vad är fel med mig?*" What is wrong with me? And Colm had known all along; he must have found out this morning. He hadn't bothered updating her on all the details, presuming Morag would tell her, if it hadn't already come up in conversation. And Colm was melancholic in solitude, realising that life really could pass you by; this wasn't a dress rehearsal, and if you didn't make an effort when the opportunity was standing in front of you, people would be gone, moving on to an alternative future. One that excluded you.

Of course she should have worked it out for herself. Morag had a new man, but was being cautious about announcing who it was. Perhaps she was worried about how friends would react in the face of this shift in the social balance. Or maybe she was taking it steady in case things went wrong. But she cared, she was worried. That was why she had called telling Ylva she had to speak to Dougie. Because Morag couldn't bear to see Dougie sad.

"I have to go home," she whispered to herself. Raising her head, she looked at herself in the mirror. The tears were still pouring from her eyes. Shit. This wind burn was bad, she told herself. Tugging her sleeve up over her wrist, she wiped at her eyes. Not perfect, but it would have to do. She wanted to be home. Regardless of what had happened last night, she couldn't think of anything she would rather do. She felt strangely embarrassed, humiliated, and incredibly out of place. Plain stupid.

Pushing the key into the ignition, she decisively fired up the engine. Get me out of here.

Later that evening Ylva was in the bath, staring at a steamy ceiling. A numb face, but no more tears. The wind had stopped. She was a little surprised by how calmly she had returned home and settled into her routines. No fear of a reprisal attack from the stranger, possibly a dead man called Tom. Her chest had been torn up and she didn't feel fear. Didn't really care. Felt drunk on too much thinking.

The thought fully occurred to her for the first time that she had to leave the island. She wanted to move away. She couldn't stay here. Live in her prison where her legs had been ripped up. She didn't want to see people she knew again. Happy people. Never again. It was a bitter twist that as his last act Dougie had decided to sabotage things with Karl. Otherwise she could have called the Swede up and suggested talks for starting a business on Gotland, Sweden. But no, Dougie had to bugger up even that.

Sinking back into the lukewarm bath water, Ylva closed her eyes. Take me away from here. I don't want to be here anymore. Why don't you join me at the burn? It's a beautiful place. His voice was in her head. She opened her eyes and she was in the bowl at the base of the Cullins, the fairy pools river cutting through the ground ahead of her.

"You're welcome to go and take a look."

The stranger was stood a little way off. The handsome man with his sculpted face and twisting, loose locks of hair.

That slightly wry smile. They had danced at the caelidh the last time she had seen him. Still wanting to show her this hidden beauty spot; share something special.

He gestured to the place ahead. "It's just up there."

Ylva started to walk, following the dirt track up through the heather. The man was following her. The sun was blazing, the colours intense. Everything was so beautiful. The track moved down a bank onto the bare rock surface on the edge of the river. Ahead there was a small waterfall, pouring from the rock level above. Ylva stepped out into the shallow pool, surprised to notice when she looked down that her feet were bare. She hadn't felt any discomfort walking barefoot through the heathers or across the stones. The water lapped around her ankles as she started to wade out into the turquoise water.

"I really love it here."

"So do I," the man agreed.

They waded out towards the waterfall, the water reaching her thighs. He gently pushed her back up against the rock wall, splash touching the side of her face. Whispering her name, he kissed her neck, and Ylva felt herself succumb. Pulling him to her.

"Why do you always disappear on me?"

"It's you who keeps leaving."

The skirts of her ball gown were ruffled, the operatic dress she had worn on Broadford bay. And she could feel his hand travelling up the side of her leg. Warmth. He bent in to kiss her neck. When he pulled back, he had become Dougie. Ylva smiled.

"I've been missing you," he said.

Ylva reached up and kissed him on the mouth.

She opened her eyes and the toothless grin met her. The man, Tom, leered at her and gripped her neck, immobilising her against the uneven rock surface. "So pretty girly," he said to her. "You think you love me?"

Ylva tried to protest. It's not you I love. Panic built. The cuts in her legs snapped open and the water seeped with blood. Tom leaned up against her, his hot breath on her face. "I'm going to tear you apart limb by limb."

Bathwater and suds waved over the edge of the bath as Ylva sat up abruptly. Shaking. Just a dream, but Jesus, so real. Standing up, she pulled a bath towel around her body. A couple of the scabs were weeping thin strands of blood, the water on her skin pulling apart the trail. Bandages lying on top of the downturned toilet lid. Her eyes ran over her legs, the circular cuts, the place where Dougie had stitched her flesh back together.

She stepped out of the bath and picked up her bandages, starting to twine them back around her thighs. And as she sat in her bathroom, something occurred to her. If Mr Jones, the old farmer, was right, and Maud and Tom really were haunting her, then that meant a lot more than just an old deranged love story was true on Skye.

Kelpie

Also known as a waterhorse or *each uisge*. Resides in a loch or a river, known to sometimes tempt or drag people into water to drown them. Can also take on human form, presenting itself as an attractive member of the opposite sex to victims, tempting its prey to come down to the water. Can not follow over moving water.

Ylva put her book aside as Helena from the tourist office approached. She was perched on a rock edge on Broadford Bay, just a little way up from the tourist office beached in a sea-front car park.

"Afternoon, Il-va" Helena called out. "You taking a break from work?"

"Just had a morning walking group for a couple of hours," Ylva told her. "I'm finished for the day, but I didn't feel like going home just yet." Across the bay she could see the Ardnish peninsula creeping out into the sea, towards the base of which sat her little rented cottage.

"Oh aye," Helena nodded. "I'd heard there'd been some nasty goings on at your place. Did I hear right that you were attacked?"

Gossip travelled frighteningly quickly, regardless of how few people were told in the beginning. Colm wasn't one for gossip, and the police and Dougie shouldn't have told anyone because of their professional connection to the incident. Yet these things had a habit of sparking. Whipping up into fire. Ylva hadn't even told her family. They were in Sweden, so wouldn't see her legs or overhear the gossip monger at the supermarket. She couldn't see the point in worrying them.

"In your own home?" Helena pressed.

"Yes," Ylva responded. "Some headcase. I don't know who. I'm all right, though," she reassured the woman. "He just cut my legs a bit."

"Cut your legs a bit?" Helena repeated, shaking her head in a what-is-the-world-coming-to manner. "And nothing else?"

Ylva glanced at her expression from the corner of her eye. That way the eyebrows went up, the nod of things we all know about but don't mention by name in polite company. She felt irritated – why was everyone so desperate to hear she'd been ravaged by some beast, raped and scandalised.

"No, Helena," she replied drolly. "I wasn't *anything-elsed* at all."

"Well, at least that's something. Although it's still terrible. And in your own home as well. And you living all on your own. I don't know how you stand to go back. I'm not surprised you're sat out here reading your book. And you're not going to stay with one of your friends for a bit?"

"It's not as bad being home on my own as I thought it would be," Ylva admitted, avoiding the main question. What had happened seemed so surreal that it was hard to equate it with her day-to-day existence in the cold daylight. Besides which, Ylva had found a thick, determined piece of wood in the back garden that she now kept by the side of her bed.

Helena felt as though she would have to find a different route to the point she was trying to dig at. Ylva obviously wasn't going to play without a considerable amount of persuasion. She changed the subject whilst she tried to come up with a new tactic. "What are you reading?"

"This?" Ylva picked up the book, passing it across. It was an A-Z of Scottish folklore and superstition. She wasn't ready to admit she believed in ghosts, spirits, fairies and everything else, but since speaking to Hamish Jones' father, she was viewing all of this in a new light. She felt she needed to come back to her old reading matter, observing from a fresh perspective.

"Scottish folklore," Helena snorted. "We sell books like this in our little place. Tourists love these books, and the further it's taken them to get to Skye, the more they seem to want to read these books." She paused, looking over at Ylva. "And you're from Sweden, so you've come a fair old way."

"But you're from Skye; you must believe some of this."

"Because I'm from Skye?" Helena laughed. "Don't be ridiculous. It's a load of old nonsense to keep the bairns in bed."

"But some people believe," Ylva said quietly.

"Some people do. My old granny did. She knew endless stories about this island; all make believe of course. I suppose it's nice enough to know the old tales, but to actually believe all that? She used to leave all sorts out for the fairies. We did wonder if she was losing the plot by the end."

"Hmmm." Ylva took the book back, gazed down at the cover. Maybe she was losing the plot as well. So frightened after what had happened; she was looking for any explanation that would make her sleep easier at night. Searching for something to distract her attention.

"You probably shouldn't be staying on your own straight after," Helena advised, as if she had a lot of experience in these matters. "Can you not go and stay with one of your friends? What about Morag, or Dougie?"

Or what about Morag *and* Dougie, Ylva thought, tinged by sourness. "Come off it, Helena, don't play coy with me. I'm sure you've heard all about it on the gossip grapevine."

"Well, yes," Helena admitted, looking mildly embarrassed for the first time. "I have heard that there was some shouting at the pub the other week. But are you two still not on speaking terms?"

Ylva shook her head.

"It's serious then?"

She nodded. Looked over at Helena. "He was spreading lies about my business. Lies about me."

This seemed to take Helena aback a little, as if it was not what she had presumed. "About your business?"

"That I'm not insured. That I take a lot of risks, no care with my visitors. That there's been a few broken bones on my tours."

"What? But you've never had any accidents like that."

"I know. And I am properly insured."

"I'm not surprised you gave him a good shouting at the pub," Helena concluded. "No more than he deserved." She gripped Ylva's arm as if she were weakening for some illness. "Has he done much damage to your business? Did he tell a lot of people these lies?"

"It doesn't seem to have affected business as I've noticed. As far as I'm aware, he only told Karl all of this nonsense."

"Karl?"

"He was in a group of Swedes I had for a week. He tripped over the doorstep when going home from the pub – after I'd dropped them all off for the night, I'll add – and twisted his ankle. I took him to Dougie to check it out…"

"Very responsible of you."

"And Dougie told him a lot of crap about me."

Helena tutted: "That's very unprofessional."

"A lot more than that," Ylva muttered, staring steadily out to sea.

"What I don't understand, though," Helena started. "Is why he did this. We all know those are blatant lies. And he always seems like a decent guy. You two have always struck me as the best of chums."

"Oh, I don't know," Ylva sighed tiredly, brushing her hair back off her face. "He hasn't tried to deny it at least. All I've had is that he's awfully sorry, did it in panic… I'm just so fed up with it all. Friends just don't do things like this to one another."

"No, they don't. So has there been any effect from what he said? Anything bad happen?"

"The Swedes left in a hurry. Like I was cursed or something. Honestly, Helena, it was just awful. They did a midnight flit, before their week's holiday was finished. I went one morning to pick them up and they were gone. No message or anything. It took me months to get one of them to reply my phone calls, emails... Then I finally got to speak to Karl and he told me what had happened."

"It seems like a very extreme reaction to what they'd been told."

"He said they didn't want to cause a scene. Swedes don't like confrontation, you know."

Helena laughed out loud. "From what I've heard, you've not got a problem with it."

"But I'm half Scottish."

"True enough," she agreed. "I'm just trying to work out what the aim was in all of this. I mean, beyond your Swedish party cutting their hols short, what actual effects has this had?"

Ylva shrugged. "None really, other than making me paranoid about what my visitors are thinking. And then I get attacked and wonder about leaving Skye permanently, but even that door's closed."

"Why's that?"

"Well, it's not really," she conceded. "Only that Karl had been talking about setting up a tour guide company on Gotland – it's a Swedish island. It was just talk, you know, nothing but idle day dreams. But I have the experience of running such a business."

"And Karl won't touch you with a barge pole now."

"No."

"So did you tell anyone else about these Godland plans?"

"No, I told you, they were just idle chatter," Ylva paused, her brow creasing for a moment. "Although Colm asked me about it the other morning. God knows how he knew. Dougie had visited him earlier…"

"And Karl had told Dougie." Helena set her hands on her lap as she concluded the tale. "Well, Il-va, I will have to be getting back to the office."

Ylva smiled wryly. "Tired of listening to my tale of woe?"

"Ach, no, don't worry. You've got to get it out of your system. Although I am a bit surprised by you."

"By me?"

"Well, Dougie has been a disgrace, there's no denying it. But as he told you, he panicked…"

"What do you mean? If he'd been calm he would have concocted his lies better?"

"Really, you're a bright girl; I'm surprised you don't see what's been going on, for it's as plain as the nose on your face." Helena paused to peer at Ylva's increasingly irritated expression. "Or maybe the penny did drop and you daren't admit it."

"Helena, don't make comments like that. I've been through the shit…"

"I know, hen," Helena said as she stood up. "And you'll figure it out soon enough, I'm sure."

She left Ylva alone on the coast line. An angry Swedish-Scottish girl. Why was she stupid? Dougie had been treacherous, for no obvious reason. Why should it be as plain as the nose on her face? Helena had sounded as though Dougie was to be pitied. Almost that Ylva should understand. That she might be complicit in it. That just wasn't fair.

Ylva looked out to the incoming tide on the beach, waves lapping at the sand. A little way into the water stood Maud. She turned to look back to land and waved at Ylva.

Ylva struggled through the following days. Her encounters, visions, episodes, or whatever they might be called, with Maud were on the violent increase, peaking at several times a day. She barely dared to raise her head for fear of seeing the woman in the near distance; boots in hand, always ready to run away. For she never came any closer; never would communicate. Tom – if that was who it had been – had not returned to the cottage. But he remained in her dreams, leering and frightening, surrounded by blood and destruction. Ylva didn't dare sleep, eventually nodding off in the small hours of the morning when her eyelids could no longer support themselves. It was difficult to be energetic and not appear neurotic when running her tours during the daylight hours.

When she woke up that Sunday morning and drew her bedroom curtains, she was surprised to see Maud sitting in her back garden. She had never been so close to Ylva. Looking away to sea, her boots lying in the grass beside her. Ylva rapped on the window to catch her attention. Maud turned her head. "Hey, you," Ylva called out. "Wait there."

She couldn't continue like this; it was draining the energy from her very existence. She wanted Maud and Tom to leave her alone – she didn't even see why they needed to torment her. Running out of the cottage in her pyjamas, she hoped to catch Maud, somehow speak to her, reason with her to cease stalking her. You're dead now. You're not supposed to be here.

The back garden was empty. She was so tired she must be imagining all of this. She was falling to pieces. Ylva trudged back to the front door, bare feet in the dew-dropped grass.

Maud stood by the van, her hand actually on the passenger door handle as if she was about to hop in for a jaunt out in the country with Ylva. She smiled encouragingly.

Ylva was ready to cry. "What do you want?"

Maud continued to smile dumbly.

"Why won't you leave me alone?" Ylva took a step towards the vehicle, and Maud skipped back like a frightened deer, hurrying up the track back to the main road. Ylva moved to follow, then remembered she was in her pyjamas with nothing on her feet. It was one thing to sit alone at home and slowly loose her mind, another to run raving through the local community in her night attire. She'd get herself locked up in a mental asylum at this rate. She smiled wryly, so tired, the thought seemed funny; locked up in Bedlam, just as they said Tom had been all those years ago.

Inside, Ylva quickly dressed, filling her rucksack full of food, maps and water, and collecting her hiking boots on the way out. Tossing everything into the van, she reversed back down onto the access road. She drove up to the main road with no destination in mind. Pausing at the junction, she looked right, then left, then right again. Further up the road, Maud stood, her hand out like a hitchhiker. Ylva drove straight into Broadford, passing by Maud without a side glance or a thought to stop.

She continued on the coastal road from Broadford to Sligachan, twisting around the rugged shore line of Skye. Now and then Maud appeared at the side of the road. Sometimes she stuck her hand out for a lift, other times she simply stood and watched Ylva drive by. Loitering like posts marking a walk.

Ylva drove through Sligachan and onwards towards the west coast. Just before the small whisky village of Carbost, Maud appeared on the high road to the left, a junction pulling up away. Ylva indicated to go left, thinking to herself that this was the road that went past the fairy pools – the river in the bowl before the Cullins – eventually ending at Glen Brittle bay.

At first she thought she had lost Maud as she rounded the corner, then she saw her, away from the road, part way along the track to the fairy pools on the Allt Coir' a' Mhadaidh river. Ylva pulled up into the empty car park on the right and switched off the engine. Quickly changing her shoes for her hiking boots, she slung the rucksack on her back, and followed Maud down the track.

Always keeping a good twenty meters ahead, occasionally glancing back to be sure Ylva was still following, Maud led the way along the track. They crossed down across the bowl, and started the steady climb up beside the river. Water cascading peacefully. Ylva didn't bother to shout after the woman. In silence they walked, separately.

The path climbed steeply, the river cutting particularly deep through the rock bed. High waterfalls, deep chasms and cracked rocks. The path didn't go too close to the water. Climbing up to the top of the bank, Ylva was surprised to see that Maud had disappeared. Disorientated, she stepped up onto a small boulder by the path, turning around to survey the land. A light breeze blew over the heather fields. Maud had gone.

"*Var har du gömt dig?*" Ylva whispered to herself. Where are you hiding? The call of the river drew her away from the path. Stepping onto the bare rock, she moved up to the edge of a rushing chasm, watching the turquoise water rush into the shadows, thousands of years of energy beating the curves and funnels in the hard stone.

Striding across the chasm, she was on something of a rocky island, embedded in the earth. Further up the river split into two, cutting chasms and winding paths down either side of her rocky outcrop before meeting again as a waterfall. The great mass of rock was in chunks moulded together from its formation; cracks formed from the weather; the ice and the sun, the floods and the pounding river. Towards the front it had cracked into two as if a giant had pummelled it with a sledge hammer. Ylva walked up to the edge and peered down at the waterfall, the drop pool far below; the glistening, glittering continuation of the river beyond.

Something down in the dank crevice caught her eye. Lost in shadows. Getting down on all fours, Ylva took her rucksack off, removing her torch from the side pocket. Flicking it on, she shone the beam down; she found Maud and this time

Maud didn't run away. A mere meter apart, Maud met her gaze. Trapped in a break in the rock.

"Jesus, Ullba," Hamish Jones of the local police constabulary huffed as he pulled himself on to his knees. "When you rang this in, you could have been a bit more specific."

Ylva watched as he scrambled upright. He had been lying flat out across the rock, waving her torch into the crevice. "I thought it was too the point," she told him. "I've found a body in the river."

"Aye, that's fair enough," Hamish said, turning around. "But you could have mentioned that he's nothing but bones. I've called the bloody mountain rescue out. I think this fella here's beyond rescuing."

Ylva wasn't quite so sure about that; the very discovery seemed to have lifted something in herself and the atmosphere. She wasn't going to tell Hamish that, even if his father did believe in ghosts. "It's a woman."

"Sorry?"

"The body down there. It's a woman."

"How can you tell?"

Ylva ran a hand across her eyebrows. "There's no brow ridge. It's a smooth curve downwards above the eye sockets."

"I didn't know you were an anthropologist."

"I'm not; my head just happens to be full of random information." That and she was convinced the body in the rocks was Maud.

"Well, you just sit tight there," Hamish told her as he stretched up to his full height. "Bones only, a body's a body and it's got to be officially reported."

"Even if it's hundreds of years old?"

"Even if it's a thousand years old. Any discovered human remains have to be reported to the police." He took his mobile out of his pocket. "I need to get some reception. I need to call off the rescue effort."

"I can usually get some reception just up there," Ylva pointed.

Whilst Hamish went to call mountain rescue back and let them know it was a false alarm, Ylva went a little way from the crevice, and sat down on the rock river bank. Unzipping her rucksack, she took out a water bottle, taking a long draught of the lukewarm water. She leant back against the rock, feeling the sun on her face. Not a sound but the steady run of the river. This was peace.

"There's someone coming up the track."

She opened one eye. Hamish was stood above her on the next level of rock, gazing out across the plains as if he was a scout on some ridiculous mission. "Probably just some tourist," she said.

"Looks like he's got a load on his back," Hamish commented. "I hope it's not mountain rescue coming to save the day. I spoke to Colm and he said he'd try and ring round everyone to call off the rescue."

Ylva sat up, raising her hand to shield her eyes from the brightness of the sun. Even at this distance she could recognise him.

On the approach he disappeared from sight as he neared the waterfall on top of which they sat. Hamish walked over to the track to greet the single walker. "Ah, Dougie, man," he said as Dougie stepped up to the top of the waterfall. "Did Colm not manage to get in touch with you?"

"Colm? He told me there was a casualty out this way."

Like a game of Chinese whispers, Ylva thought.

Dougie visibly halted, seeing Ylva sat on the rock. He blanched a little. "Have you had an accident?"

Hamish glanced back over at her. "No, it's not Ullba; she's fine. She's the one who called it in. But I'm afraid you're too late."

"Already? I got here as fast as I could."

"Go take a look for yourself," Hamish passed him Ylva's torch. "Over there," he pointed at the crevice. "Shine a light and have a good look down."

Dougie looked a little bemused, but accepted the torch. Shrugging off his rucksack, he walked over to the crevice, squatting before flicking the light on and looking down into the shadows. Ylva watched in silence from a distance. Whatever she did, wherever she went, he just kept turning up. She had to admit, she felt calmer than on previous occasions, and had no wish to throw things at him. She just felt achingly sad. She couldn't remain like this for the rest of her life. And it made her feel even worse to think that she would have to move on.

"Do you think there's anything you can do for him?" Hamish jested.

"A decent burial," Dougie muttered. "Jesus, you need the county pathologist out; not the bloody mountain rescue. I'm here in my volunteer cap, you understand."

"Aye, but you could give us the benefit of your medical expertise. What do you think the cause of death was?"

"Malnutrition," Dougie said dryly. "I couldn't tell you from here. Although it looks as though there's quite a lot of cranial damage." He directed the beam towards the top and back of the skull. There were severe cracks and indentations; even a section of skull missing. "It might have been sustained during the fall down there; maybe rocks falling down afterwards. Or maybe it was caused prior."

"You mean he was murdered?"

"I can't say anything," Dougie replied. "Although it looks like a female skull."

"That's what Ullba said. Something about the eyebrows."

"Oh." Dougie switched off the torch and glanced across at Ylva. She looked down at her hiking boots.

"I wonder if she's been down there a long time," Hamish continued. "It's a surprise no one's noticed before now. Although if there were rocks covering her and they've only just been washed away," he drifted off thoughtfully. "Anyway, I've phoned the pathologist. There's none based on the island. You'll stay and give a hand? We might need some help getting the body out of there."

"Sure, I can help," Dougie shrugged.

Hamish turned back to Ylva. "How did you come to be looking down there, then Ullba? You don't notice it without the torch. Were you just having a poke about? Planning some new feature for your tourists?"

She looked him steadily in the eye. "I was following Maud."

He looked as though he didn't understand for a moment, then grew silent. He might have taken it for a joke if it weren't for the expression on her face and what he had seen of her legs the other night. "You went and spoke to my father?"

"I did."

Dougie stood up. "Who's Maud?"

"A dead woman." Hamish stepped away from the final resting place of what they presumed was Maud's. He strode past Ylva and onto the next step of rock. "It'll be a wee while before the pathologist shows his face, but I'll have to stay with the body now. Are you all right to wait?" he asked Dougie.

"Sure."

"You can head off if you like," he said to Ylva. "I don't know whether we'll need a statement as such – I doubt this will become a police matter – but I know where to find you if we do."

"Yes, I think I will." She put the empty water bottle back in her rucksack. Dougie still had her torch in his hand, but she didn't want to ask for it back.

Hamish watched her as she shouldered her rucksack. "You know, if you're right about that, things should calm down for you now," he told her. "I think you'll have done what needed to be done."

"I hope so."

Ylva started back down the track in the long distant direction of the car park. She was warmed by the sun, but her body was tired. The adrenaline was switching off and she needed to rest. As much as she ought to savour a day like this, she just wanted to go home and sleep. Hurried footsteps soon joined the rhythm of the river. She paused, turning slightly to look back up the path. Dougie was following her, torch in hand.

"Ylva." He came to a halt in front, awkward and a little wary. "You forgot your torch."

She accepted it, holding it down by her side. "Thank you." An uncomfortable silence formed. She wished she could just disappear. Something held her back. Dougie looked as though he was on the verge of saying something. Anger had dispersed, replaced by disappointment over what had been done, how things had worked out. "I'd better head back…"

"Look, Ylva," he blurted as she turned to leave. "Can I have a wee word?"

She wanted to make some kind of response, but her throat just tightened. Was he going to tell her about Morag now?

Dougie stared back at her and looked as though there were a hundred things he wanted to say that he still couldn't quite word. "You keeping well?"

She almost coughed up surprise. What was wrong with him? Polite conversation as if literally nothing had happened. "I'm fine."

"I mean after what happened the other night. He's not been back? Because I don't know what I'd…"

"There's nothing to worry about," she told him. "I'm fine. But I'm very tired. I've not been sleeping well recently and I want to get home."

Polite civilities. There was nothing worse. "Aye, you get away home. Look after yourself."

"Bye then."

Dougie watched as she turned and started along the path again. A solitary figure, torch in hand. "I just wish things could get back to the way they were before."

Ylva felt herself crumble like water. She stubbornly continued forward, her eyes filling up with tears. Don't we all wish so.

It was surprising how much your perspective could change after a few days of really good rest. The calm would envelope. Anger had vanished. *C'est la vie*, and I am smiling about it.

She had not seen Maud again. Wherever Maud had been trying to get to, she had arrived. She didn't need to stalk Ylva now. Her dreams were peaceful too, and Tom was absent, presumably banished under Maud's departure; for the connection had been broken. Her legs were healing and Ylva had her life back.

She'd finished a two-day walking tour with a group of spritely Dutch travellers. The first day had been quite wet, and although the weather hadn't stopped the walkers or lessened their enthusiasm, it had muddied their boots, and in turn Ylva's minibus. The mud dried, and she didn't keep a finicky clean transport, but she had certain standards. Now that the tour was complete, she was back home tidying up the mess. She'd taken the mats out of the van, and was whacking them in turn on the corner of the garden wall to shake the dried earth free.

A figure was walking down their no-through road: they sometimes got tourists walking down here to go out to the headland to bird watch. Ylva didn't give the passerby any attention until they stopped, backed a little and walked up to her cottage.

"Ylva."

She paused in her cleaning, her hair tousled and her face a little pink from the exertion. She was surprised: both that Dougie was stood on her drive; but more so that she didn't feel like hitting him, shouting at him or throwing around threats and general terms of abuse. She didn't know quite how to behave. "Dougie," she responded as she straightened.

He shrugged his shoulders as if lost for words. "I was just taking a walk; ended up coming down here without thinking."

"Oh." It didn't exactly sound positive. "I see." Maybe he wanted to continue his walk, had hoped to ignore her, then felt he ought to go up and say hello. "It's a nice day for it," she offered, a rather pathetic attempt at conversation.

"Aye." He took a breath as if there was more to say, then changed his mind. "I'd better let you get back to your mat beating."

Ylva dropped the mat as he started back down her drive. "Dougie?"

He halted, looked back.

"I'd prefer to have everything cleared up, you know? I don't want to not understand." Be left with the same questions for the rest of her life, a collection of regrets whenever she thought of Skye, bundled up in her Swedish cottage in the forests, or wherever it was that she would eventually end up.

"Understand?"

She felt apologetic, as if she had no right to ask these things. "Why you told Karl what you did? I don't understand why you wanted to sabotage me."

"I didn't; I don't. It's the last thing I'd want to do." He lingered indecisively on the road for a moment before walking back up her drive. "I just panicked. It was a stupid, stupid thing to do, and I…"

"But why did you tell Karl those lies?"

Dougie looked at her. "Because he was being so annoying."

This sounded farcical. "Karl annoyed you so you told him shit about me?"

"No. Well, I suppose yes. Ylva, you weren't in there whilst I was checking his ankle. Jesus, he was such an idiot. He was telling me about his life as if I cared, and about his plans and this business he was going to set up with you. On some Swedish island or something, I don't remember all of the details."

"So you let him think I was a crap businesswoman," Ylva finished. "For your information, those *plans* hadn't gotten beyond a slightly intoxicated conversation one evening. Karl's just trapped in a life he never asked for and needs his daydreams to keep him going. But do you know what; in telling him that, you effectively cut off my future chance of steady income back home."

"It would have meant you leaving Skye."

She felt a little exasperated. "But you must realise that will happen sooner or later anyway. Nothing stays the same, and at the end of the day I do not belong here. Everyone knows this is just some interim in my life, and as much as I don't want to think about it, I know deep down that I can't keep bumbling on through life like this. I'm going to have to get some permanence; a proper home rather than just renting someone else's holiday cottage…" the words poured out, surprising even Ylva, and saddening her to admit that this comfortable existence wouldn't go on forever. Things were constantly changing, the dynamics of people's lives altered. Grew, broke apart, merged. "Things change. Look at you and Morag."

"What about me and Morag?"

His expression wasn't exactly the tender look of wistful new love, more of irritation. Ylva didn't feel on quite so steady ground. Perhaps they'd had a lovers' tiff. She sat down at the back of her van where the two doors were open. "Well, new relationships and things…"

"What are you on about? Maybe Morag's having a grand old time – maybe not the way she's being so coy and no one's allowed to know who he is; maybe he's just a figment of her imagination."

This didn't sound right. "So you're not…?"

"Not what?"

Dougie looked angry. Was he the spurned lover? Ylva didn't dare ask. "Nothing."

"And as for me, I'm stuck in some kind of bloody limbo, and instead of moving things forward, I seem to manage to screw things up in classic style. I make you think I'm out to get you, even though I'm not. You won't even speak to me…"

"I'm speaking to you now."

"Aye," he sighed. "You're speaking to me, and I should be thankful for that." He sat down next to her in the van. "But

I've messed things up with you in a grand old way. And things won't get back to what they were."

She felt awful, as if everything over the past few weeks was all her fault. "Look, I've calmed down a lot..." she started.

"And really, I don't even want to go back to that."

"Oh." She leant back from him. Perhaps he'd been disappointed by her aggressive, child-like reaction to the original news of the betrayal. You're not the friend, the decent sort of person I thought you were and all of that. She stuck her hands into her sweater pockets, her fingers touching crumpled paper.

"You know I'd been planning on going back to Lewis for a wee break?" he continued. "I've just been feeling so shit after it all came out. I wanted to get away from all of this. And then I got called out one night because this girl had gotten herself cut up by some roaming nutter." He glanced across at her. "Jesus, Ylva, you do not know how worried I've been. And you isolating yourself off out here with that fucking psycho wandering free."

"Aw, Dougie," she said. Taking her hands from her pockets, still holding the paper, she linked arms with him. "I never knew you cared so much."

"Don't josh with me, Ylva." He pushed her off.

Åh gud. It clicked into place. Admit it to yourself, girl, because he is being honest. She couldn't look at him. Down at her hands. Crumpled paper in her fingers. A note from Dougie, written shortly after this had first blown up. Balled up in anger, not quite thrown to the sea. Crinkled noise as she broke it apart, eyes flickering over the words. And she understood. Him, her, the fear of change. Even greater, the fear of rejection. Uncertainty. She'd been using Morag as a personalised smoke screen. And it wasn't the wind that made her cry. No one wanted to leave. "Dougie?"

"What?"

She didn't quite know what to say. Rather she knew exactly what she wanted to say, but couldn't find the courage to speak as she wished. She didn't know how to behave around him anymore. "Do you want to come for a walk along the beach?"

He looked as though she were mad, but agreed with a grunt. Ylva pushed the van doors to as they left her cottage and walked down to the sea front. It was a quick step up onto the seawall, then a short jump onto the rocks on the other side. Gently moving across down to the sand. Dougie stuck his hands into his jacket pocket and marched stubbornly onwards as if he was walking on his own, had to get somewhere quickly. He looked so serious, in fact, possibly depressed. It didn't make her feel particularly good, considering he'd as good as admitted those words of desire. To then look as if the world was a wicked, dark place was not exactly a compliment.

"Will you cheer up?" Ylva said, acting before thinking and pushing him into the sea for want of anything better to do.

"Jesus, Ylva!" Dougie shouted, stumbling in a half-moon through the dying waves, salt water splashing up his trouser leg. "What was that in aid of?"

She hooked her hands on her jeans pockets and shrugged nonchalantly. "You just looked so serious."

"And would you like it if I threw you in the sea?" He grabbed at her wrist and pulled her across the sand.

"No!"

He relented a little, making no move to push her into the sea, but not letting go of her arm either. "I'm sorry, Ylva, but I can't do this."

"Can't do what?"

"I can't be mates with you like we were before. It was hellish when you weren't speaking to me, but I can't sit and watch whilst your Swedish laddy boy…   "

"Then don't." She stepped up to him to speak to his ear. The breeze cut out from the shelter of his body. "I think there's been a mistake. There is no Swedish laddy boy. There never was."

Dougie twisted his neck a little to look at her. "Are you teasing me?"

"Hardly." She tilted up and kissed him. He barely responded. Christ, she thought, suddenly feeling uncertain.

Had she got the wrong end of the stick? Again? "You'd tell me if I was doing something wrong?"

He didn't say anything. Just smiled and kissed her; still holding onto her arm so she couldn't get away. And that was answer enough.

Dougie stayed with her. In the evening she had taken him into her bed. At night they'd woken, dressed and gone out for a walk by the coast, the summer light still lingering, only just and barely discernable, but there.

They'd returned to the cottage, dropping back to sleep on the bed, fully clothed. Ylva lay on her side, watching Dougie sleep. It was silly how awkwardness, even embarrassment and a terrible fear of rejection and maybe even change had kept all of this in limbo for who knew how long.

Smiling to herself, Ylva rolled over. A face smiled back at her, and for a moment she thought Dougie had woken up, until the low laugh beat out in steady rhythm and she realised that Dougie was actually in the bed behind her.

"Hello there, girly," Tom's toothy grin stretched wide. "Thought you'd gotten rid of me?"

Ylva had a moment to indulge in nausea panic before Tom grabbed a fistful of her hair and pulled her head-first out of the bed with him. It was terrifying how quickly the adrenaline started, the force of her heart so hard against her ribs, trying to jump ship. She tried to twist around, call out for, reach for Dougie, but he was fast asleep and oblivious. Another world.

Because it was all true. Old mad Tom was really here. She thought he had gone when Maud had, but clearly that wasn't so. She couldn't think why he had waited to come back.

"Come on, I've got work to do," he said, hauling her through into the darkened living room.

But the grasp of his hand on her hair, the sound and the solid angle of his body said otherwise – this wasn't a ghost, this was a real man. Just a roaming psychopath. "Who are you?"

He pushed her against the back of the settee. "You know who I am, lassie. Tom."

"As in Maud's"

His cracked lips stretched.

Ylva glanced across at the bedroom doorway. Why wasn't Dougie waking up? "Why didn't you just finish this the other night?"

"I like them to be awake. Maud'll tell you that. You two are such good friends." He pushed himself up against her. "I'll start with your legs; scrape the flesh from your bones. You don't know the meaning of screaming."

Was he a mad man or was he a ghost? She didn't know which and she didn't know what to do. How to defend herself. But if he was solid, if he could hurt her, surely it was a mutual highway of reaction under action. She wasn't going to die like this, the victim of some long-festering madness. Ylva kneed him in the groin, wriggling free, tripping away as he tried to grab at her. Where now? She didn't know where to go, what to do. She ran to the front door, unlocking it and fleeing out into the blackness.

Groaning, Tom pulled himself back up to his full height, hands grasping the back of the settee. He had his knife, laid across the top of the settee, pushed into the palm of his hand as his fist clenched. He didn't notice the drool of blood dripping on the carpet.

"Come back here, you harlot!" he shouted, staggering towards the front door. "I'm going to cut you up. Pluck an eyeball and let you see," he cackled. Moving out onto the doorstep, looking out onto the night. Where was she?

"Right here." Ylva loomed up from the exterior wall, swinging the old fence post like a golf club. The wood met neatly with the back of Tom's head, a heavy vibration rippling through the length of his body. A dull thud, a crunch, his head jerking up, eyes rolling in their sockets and he slumped down to the ground, blood on his lips.

Working quickly, Ylva unlocked the van and pulled out a coil of rope. Tying his legs and arms behind his back, she soon had him trussed like a chicken. For if he could take this form and hurt her, it worked both ways and she was at liberty to defend herself. The only problem, she thought to herself as she dragged his wiry body, belly-down, across to the van, was what was she going to do with him now. In the here and now there was nothing to be done, because he didn't exist, certainly not in a legal or rational sense. She couldn't take him anywhere to be locked up, and she couldn't ask the authorities for protection.

This had to end. She couldn't kill him, because he was already dead. She didn't know whether chopping him up, as he'd threatened to do with her, would work, but Ylva doubted she could stomach a task quite so gruesome. Pulling him up into the back of the van, she collapsed on one of the passenger seats and looked at his unconscious form. What to do with a dead man who wasn't going away? If she'd believed in heaven and hell, she'd know he wasn't going to heaven for what he was. But likewise it didn't seem that the devil was able to accept him into hell either, regardless of his repeated performance of Taghairm.

Stepping over him, she slammed the doors shut and glanced back at the house, a little wistfully. Dougie hadn't woken. She didn't suppose he would at the moment. This was somewhere else, disconnected from her real life.

Walking around to the driver's seat, she pulled herself into the van. What to do with Tom? She would have to play him at his own game, at his own version of existence. Find a way to get him off her back; permanently. Think, Ylva. Folklore and ghost stories. And if one was true, were all the other stories true as well?

She glanced over her shoulder at his crumpled shape in the gloom. It was just a case of finding someone or something nasty enough to be able to take Tom on. Something stronger, potentially more vicious, that could take care of a mere mad little ghost like Tom. A ghost who was once just a mortal man.

Ylva put the key in the ignition. Not only was there something capable, but she had already met it on more than one occasion.

The drive through the night Skye wilderness was mostly silent. Not another vehicle on the roads. Dawn just beginning to approach in the small hours. Steady away, Ylva calmed herself, you have your plan and you'll get there in good time.

When she pulled up into the empty parking area, Tom was starting to come around. She flung open the doors, tightening her fingers around the ropes to drag him roughly from her van, dropping like a rock to the ground. Tom groaned.

"Rise and shine," she crouched, untying his legs but leaving his arms secured behind his back. She slung the remainder of the rope casually around his neck and shoulders as if it were a fashion accessory. "We're going for a walk."

Tom tumbled onto his feet. Ahead were the Cullin Mountains, cast in early morning shadows. The light was thin, hard to see. Ahead, before the mountains, was a bowled plain, a burn, hardly visible, cutting through. Somewhere up there in the distant mountainous backdrop was his cave of gold.

His teeth were bloodied, but he smiled. "Maud," he whispered, recognising the battered girl's final resting place. Pushed into a crack high up in the river, covered over with heavy rocks so that she might not be found. Never to have a final resting place, to walk lost forever, a tormented toy to track. Oh the screams, the blood, the jerking of her body, even when he thought she could take no more.

Ylva pushed him forward.

"We're going to play?"

"You are."

They crossed the road and followed the path down to the river. Ylva was always behind, her eyes steadily focused on Tom. She carried her fence post over her shoulder, ready to give him a poke when he tried to veer, twist to look back at her. Thinking this was a game he could still win. Crossing over a small stream, they started up the side of the fairy pools river, the sound strong in the silence, the glint of water creeping through. Ylva's eyes started to wander, worry building. What if she had been wrong? What would she do with Tom then? What if he wasn't here?

"I don't know what you think you're going to do with me," Tom laughed. "I'm not afraid."

He was sat on a boulder beside the river, a hand thoughtfully propping up his head as he gazed into the running water.

Ylva and Tom stopped on the track running up by the river. Tom looked from the man to Ylva and laughed. "You brought me to your play mate?"

The man stood up and looked directly at Ylva. "You're back?"

The light was incredibly poor, but she could see his sculpted features perfectly. The tousled chestnut hair. Piercing eyes. A face, physique and a stare that made a girl forget herself. "I've brought you a present," Ylva said, giving Tom a prod as if he were cattle. "Someone for the river."

"You want rid of him," the man pointed out.

"He's already dead. No one wants him. You'll have him for eternity."

Tom laughed; it sounded as though he was a little irritated at being ignored. Talked about as if he wasn't there. "Who's the play mate?"

Ylva pushed Tom in the small of the back. He stumbled through the heather to the edge of the bare rock river back. As he tripped away from her, she spoke quietly: "You should know."

The man tilted his head, took a step back into the river. The rush of water didn't appear to affect him. His eyes flashed. "He can come down to the river."

A memory; perhaps a spark of recognition. Old tales by the fireside at night. Grandmother's warning. The kelpie. Tom's smile dropped.

"Take him then!" Ylva warded Tom away with the fence post as he tried to scramble back up towards her.

The kelpie held his arms wide open as if to say he wasn't to blame. He was stood in the middle of the river. "I can't do everything," he said. "You'll have to bring him to me."

Her body closed up in fear. "But you'll drown me."

"Now, now," he scolded her. "If you don't bring him, he'll never leave you alone."

"No!" Tom shouted. His shoulders writhed, trying to break free of the rope. Scrambling at the bank. She couldn't let him go. Dropping the fence post, Ylva pushed at Tom, striding down to the rock face and taking a hand hold on the knotted ropes. He pulled and strained, but she dragged him to the water. This had to end. Tom was screaming. At the water edge.

"Here."

"You have to bring him in the water."

"I can't."

He dropped his arms. "I don't bite."

Tom jerked, running away from the river, almost popping Ylva's arms from their sockets. Like a wild dog on a lead. She pulled him back, heaving him into the water. A loud splash, water waving and crashing up around the mad man's legs. The kelpie came for him. Ylva was set off balance as she slipped on the wet, submerged rocks, unnerved by Tom's shouts, pulling at the ropes. The ice-cold water soaked into her clothing, making it heavy like chains. Rushing and roaring and suddenly it was up over her head. Tom was disappearing into the murky depths of the water, screaming and waving, tied on the back of a bucking horse. Something was pulling down on her shoulders. Ylva struggled to fight it off, aware of the river surface far above her. She'd never realised the river was this deep. And she could see his face, those beautiful eyes, the wholeness enveloping her. It was too much and she had to breathe. She opened her mouth and the water poured in. Her body started to jerk into spasms. The kelpie smiled.

She slapped the side of her face. "Wake up there, hen." No response. An exasperated sigh. "I didn't pull you out for nothing. And I know you can hear me."

Ylva opened her eyes. The woman smiled at her. A stranger. She didn't know where she was. She opened her mouth, surprised to be coughing on fresh air.

"Steady there," the woman advised. "You've had a bit of a shock."

"Where am I?" Ylva spoke hoarsely, sitting up abruptly and feeling the blood rush from her head. She was on a grassy patch away from the river, the fairy pools river. Full morning, but it was clouded over; the light having something of a silver sheen. The woman sat back on her heels. A Scottish woman of no obvious age, a slightly bulbous nose and a calm face. Her long, dark-blonde hair was tousled and ragged, seemingly tied here and there with thin velvet ribbons which twisted and hung in amongst her hair. She was wearing what looked like layers of shift dresses, something from a medieval fancy dress party.

Ylva looked from the woman to the river. The kelpie had pulled her under. "You pulled me out?"

The woman nodded. "Oh aye."

"You rescued me. I was drowning."

"You did drown."

Ylva couldn't look away from the river. "And is he?"

The stranger raised an eyebrow. "Is he? Do you mean the kelpie? He's still in there. Don't worry yourself over it, though," she patted Ylva's arm. "He won't be after you now."

"And what about Tom?"

The woman tinkled with laughter. "He's still in there. I wasn't going to waste my energy pulling out a fellow like him."

It was surreal. She had almost died. Tom could have brought her down. This stranger had saved her, passing by for who knew what reason. Sheer luck, because at that time in the morning, there ought not to have been any passers by at all. "Thank you," she said to the woman. "I was very lucky you were passing."

"Och, now," the woman waved off the compliment. "Luck had nothing to do with it. I couldn't let you drown in there with him. And you've always shown your respects. One good turn deserves another. She always showed her respects as well, come to think of it."

"Who?"

"Maud."

"Maud?" Ylva stared at the woman, feeling a little uncomfortable in her company. "Who did you say you were?"

"I didn't. But I know you. Whenever you've been by you've always left an offering. And don't think these things go by unnoticed. Because they don't."

"Always left an offering?"

"Fairy glen."

"Fairy glen?" Ylva's voice screamed of disbelief.

The woman smiled in good humour. "You've been stalked by a ghost; attacked by a dead man; drowned by a kelpie, but you don't believe in fairies? I find that a little bit hard to believe."

Rescued by fairies. Maybe she was hallucinating. It had been a very stressful day. Week. Month. Ylva felt a sob catch in the back of her throat. She wanted to go home now. Back to Dougie. "I have to get back," she said as she stood up. "Dougie'll worry."

The woman hopped to her feet as well. "I think there's been a misunderstanding."

Ylva looked ahead. Then she turned around and looked up at the Cullin Mountains as if they shouldn't be there. Turned 180 degrees again to face the Cullins. She was fenced in by mountains and this wasn't right. There was supposed to be a gentle bowl, then a path up to the car park. It was all gone. "What's going on?"

"You see, when I heard the kelpie had got you, I thought: I can't let this happen. To leave you in there for eternity. A kelpie's play thing."

Ylva rounded on the woman. "Oh god," she moaned. "You said I drowned."

The fairy looked to the ground.

"I drowned in there," she waved an arm at the river. "You're saying I'm dead?"

The fairy wouldn't look at her.

"What is this place?"

"It's the other side. You've read about it in your books. Where we live."

She was dead. She was on the other side of existence. Ylva gazed across the weird landscape; the strange light. Of course it all made sense. The ring of mountains suddenly hemming her in. Everything was surreal. Across the heather she could see a small girl hunched up crying. She had no idea what kind of mythical creature that was supposed to be. But she didn't care. She didn't want to die just yet. This was too early. There were still things she had to do. She had only just made it up with Dougie. It couldn't be the end of relations already. Ylva felt her eyes brim up with tears. This wasn't fair.

"I know you don't think it's fair," the fairy told her. "But there are good things. You're coming to live with us in the fairy glen. It's a good place." She pointed across to the mountains that were new additions to the landscape Ylva had once known. "There's a cave up there, our entrance to the fairy glen. Follow me and I'll show you."

The fairy started down her path. Ylva robotically followed, tears falling down her face. Dripping to the ground, marking her tracks. She wasn't ready to be dead, yet here she was. So much missed.

As they made their way across to the foot of the mountains, Ylva became aware of a sniffling sound that was not her own. She wiped her eyes, held her breath for a moment to check. Someone else was definitely crying. She stopped and looked back. Twenty meters or so behind the little girl stopped as well. She was sobbing. Her expression suggested she didn't want to be with them, but was stubbornly following. She looked away as if she wouldn't meet Ylva's eye.

The fairy back tracked to Ylva.

"Who is that?"

"Just ignore her," the fairy advised. "We'll soon lose her when we go through the mountain."

Ylva was a little reluctant. The sobbing drove into her. But she turned away and did as she was told, following the fairy along the track. Soon the heather petered out, and low-lying scree built up on the surface. They began to climb steadily upwards. The small pebbles became rocks became boulders. The light glared. It was like walking on the moon. Ahead, in the shadows of the crevices and peaks of the mountain she could see the dark opening of a cave.

"Look," called the fairy. "There's our cave."

Ylva stumbled over a rock. "Ow." She sat down on a boulder, putting her ankle on her knee. There didn't appear to be any damage. Looking up, she saw that the child had squatted down amongst the rocks. Watching. There was something familiar about her that she couldn't quite place. Dark, slightly waved hair down to her shoulders. A simple red top and blue trousers. "Who is she?"

The fairy glanced coolly in the girl's direction. "Just some dead child. Don't worry about her."

"Shouldn't we take her with us?"

"No."

"But we could?"

The fairy shrugged.

Ylva looked back to the girl. A little dead child. "Will you come up here?" she called out. The girl shook her head. "You don't want to stay out here on your own?"

"I'm not coming!" the little girl shrieked in a distinctly Scottish accent. Her face turned red as if she were about to throw a tantrum. "I'm not going with her."

"I told you," the fairy said simply. "Don't bother with her."

Ylva looked back at the girl. So familiar. Maud, she thought. Are you the girl Maud?

"Are you coming?" the fairy asked.

"No," Ylva replied, surprised how easily and unexpectedly the answer came. "Not just yet. I want to look at the mountains."

They sat for an arbitrary length of time. Time had no meaning, yet the sun still traversed the sky. The fairy perched a little higher up the slope, humming to herself and playing with her ribbons as she waited for Ylva. Further down the mountain, the child curled up and went to sleep for a few hours, apparently calming. Ylva rested.

It wasn't until the fairy asked if they shouldn't go to the glen now, that everything started to break. The little girl woke up, scrambling from her bed of rocks, immediately bursting into tears again. Ylva felt nauseous. She looked over her shoulder at the fairy. We can't leave her here like this.

The fairy's face soured. "Leave her."

"Will you not come with us?" Ylva called out.

The girl shook her head.

"Leave the little dead girl," the fairy said quietly.

She wasn't sure what drove her; a gush of humanity or a need to drag someone else equally traumatised through to the other side with her like a security blanket. But Ylva walked down towards the girl. The girl looked more alert, her sobbing ceasing as Ylva neared. Stopping a few metres away, she dropped into a crouch. "Maud," she said to the girl. "Come with us."

The child's eyes narrowed. "I'm not Maud."

Not Maud. Well, it had only been a guess. It was just that there was something familiar about her.

"Who are you?"

"Me."

Ylva looked irritated. This wasn't the time for stupid games. But at least the girl wasn't crying anymore. "All right," she started, coming at it from a different angle. "What's your name?"

"You decide."

"Leave her," the fairy shouted.

"Look, you don't want to stay out here on your own, do you? Come with us to the other side."

"I'm not going with her."

"Fine," Ylva stood up. "Then you'll stay here on your own."

The little girl hesitated as Ylva marched back up the scree towards the fairy. She stumbled forward a little, then stopped. She was trembling, panicking. "She's a liar!" she screeched at Ylva's back. "I'm not dead."

"What does she mean?" Ylva looked over to the fairy, who shrugged, a little sheepish. "Who is she?"

"What does it matter?"

"I don't want to play your games. Not yours. Not hers." She broke out into a run, thundering down the mountain side. The little girl yelped and started to run away. Ylva wasn't taking anymore of this nonsense. She pursued, grabbing out at the little girl and picking her up on the run. "You tell me what this is about." She lost her balance, stumbling backwards with the weight of the child in her arms, landing on the rocks.

"She's lying. I'm not dead." The child writhed, twisting around to look at Ylva. "Neither are you."

"What?"

"Close your eyes." Small hands came up to her face, pulling down her eyelids. Suddenly she was in darkness. A dark room. No, dimmed. Lights far away. There was a steady sound. An upwards and downwards hiss. A regular electronic beat. There was a man close by. He was checking something. Thinking. I wonder if she's registered on the organ donation scheme.

Ylva pulled away sharply. Horrified. "You're not dead," the girl whispered.

"Is this true?" She scrabbled around on the rocks, looking up the slope to the fairy. "Is it true what she says?"

The fairy shrugged. "I never actually said you were dead."

"I drowned."

"They resuscitated you," the girl said.

"Touch and go," the fairy drawled. "Look, you'll not get this opportunity again. Come across with me."

Ylva looked around, feeling tugging on her arm. The child's fingers were digging into her flesh. "You're not dead," the girl reminded her. "Let's go home. You come with me." She wiped at her red eyes and her runny nose as if to make herself presentable. Stood up and took Ylva's hand in hers. "Let's go.

It was as if she was the youngest now, needing guidance. Ylva stood up and started to walk back down the mountain with the young girl. Behind her she could hear the fairy giggling. "Never mind," the fairy called after her. "No hard feelings, my dear Ylva. I just hope she doesn't annoy you too much!"

She felt the girl's hand tighten around her fingers. "*Lämna inte mig*," the girl whispered. She looked terrified. Don't leave me.

"*Lämna inte mig?*"

Ylva opened her eyes and took her first unaided breath for that day.

Afterword

The song *Bedlam Boys* is an old traditional English folksong.

The Skye legend of old mad Tom and the unrequited love of Maud is a product of my imagination and bears no resemblance to people living or dead, although there are elements borrowed from other legends and folktales from Skye. References to other legends are pulled from folklore, and if this interests you, I can recommend Otta Swire's book *Skye: The Island and its Legends*. Although if you've found yourself at all interested by the Isle of Skye, really the best thing to do would be to get yourself on the most appropriate form of transport and go there.

Lovers of Old Films
Ophelia Finsen

Fresh from university and eager for the rest of his life, Edward Gable moves to York to start a position in a graduate training scheme. And whilst real life may not meet his expectations, the building he moves into can more than compensate for the lack of excitement. Certainly everyone is friendly and helpful, but there are secrets no one wants to talk about – and if you find yourself living in a building with Sophia Loren, you know something out of the ordinary is going to happen.

Ever wanted to be your idol?

Society of Lost Causes
Ophelia Finsen

In a small town in the Yorkshire Dales there is a select gathering known as the Society of Lost Causes. A gathering of eccentric and unknown people; people who feel that they or their work will have no consequence for the world. Until a murder without motive is committed in their small community, and three potential witnesses are drawn together permanently through the twist and turns of a crime scene and an organisation dedicated to remembering contemporary and historical oddities.

This is a tale of the joy of story-telling; of the fascination in the detail and the small curiosities of life that are there for anyone to find if they are only prepared to stop and listen.

Only One Way
Jannicke Howard

What is the HEMO10 Virus? This is a completely new disease... It is a hemorrhagic fever... It is a violent and aggressive virus... We do not know where it originated... There is no vaccine or cure...

When restrictions on travel between counties are suddenly imposed in the United Kingdom, the residents of York don't worry too much, despite the rumours seeping out via the international media. It's only when a complete ban on travel and martial law is brought in, that people start to panic; and see first hand for themselves just what the world's governments and health organisations have been hoping could have been avoided. For this is a virulent and very sudden pandemic.